Pure Evil

Sasha Olympus

Contents

Chapter 1

I moved around the crowded strip club with a tray of drinks. Tonight the club was filled with men who were in the mood to blow their cash. I wasn't one of the strippers, I was simply a waitress. The girls who took off their clothes tended to walk out of here with thousands in their pockets while I only got a couple hundred. I'll take what I could get. The club was owned by the Inferno MC and they were one of the baddest clubs in the country. They had chapters in several cities, taking up damn near half the state. Their base where the president lived was only a few blocks away, so if shit went down the trouble makers had to deal with either him, the VP, or their third. Many of the bikers stayed away from the strip club, not wanting to get tangled in stripper pussy, and I don't blame them. The girls were heartless, back stabbing, bitches who would do anything to make their wallets heavier.

The club was ran by a man named Carlos who was a greedy bastard that was taking a cut of everyone's checks, and even selling the girls on the side. One of the girls had wanted to go to Inferno and tell them what Carlos has been doing, and he found out. Haven't seen her since. It was warning enough to all of us that worked here, snitches will need more than stitches.

I was on my way back to the bar when I noticed three bikers come into the bar, Inferno patches on their backs. I smirked to myself, shit was gonna go down tonight and I couldn't wait. When no one was looking I slipped out the back to the alley where Carlos had a door that was his emergency exit for when shit went south. The door opened out into the alley so I had to find a way to block it. I then saw a long rod. It was heavy but I managed to lift it and put it so it wwas being held up between the door and the building next door. No matter how hard he pushes on his door, he won't be able to get out. I smiled then slipped back into the building.

Immediately after all patrons were gone, Inferno put the club on lock down. I sat on the bar with a beer, wishing I had some popcorn. Carlos came out of his office then his eyes widened when he saw them. He ran back to his office and I had suppress my laughter when I heard his curses. They went in and dragged him out. They forced him to sit down and all the women to sit on the stage.

"Do you know who I am," One of them asked him. He was a big guy that spelled of danger and fun. Well, at least what I considered fun. "You're Hades," Carlos answered, while sweating like a pig. "The VP of Inferno." "Wrong, I'm now the President. When I looked through our finances I saw a lot of money missing from here," He answered coldly. "Care to tell me where it is?" I became giddy and couldn't wait for his answer.

"I've had repairs and other things come up," Carlos tried. I began to laugh coldly, "Damn Carlos, if you're gonna lie, give him something that's at least a little convincing." Hades crossed his arms as he looked at me, "And you are?" "The name is Vixen, but here they call me Crimson. I'm then waitress and bartender since Carlos wanted an all female staff to bring in more money. As you saw while these beautiful ladies were shaking their asses, money is no problem here." I got off the bar and walked over to them, placing a hand on Carlos's shoulder, "You see Carlos here has been stealing from not only you guys, but us women too. Every check for the last two years of mine, has always been between three hundred and four hundred short. I get the slips and it says one fifty for taxes which is normal, but that three hundred to four hundred is, poof, gone. Now I had a conversation with Carlos and he told me if I truly wanted to earn back that money then I had to put out." I chuckled darkly as my grip tightened, "Yet, even if I did, I wouldn't have made that back, instead he would've taken more. You see, he sells these poor girls, to deep his pockets. We actually had a girl named Heart, at least that was her stripper name. She wanted to go and tell you boys about the drugs, the money, and the women being used. Carlos here found out and to say he was pissed is the understatement of the year. We haven't seen her since." Carlos was crying out in pain now, yet I kept going. "We all have an idea of what happened to her, so it convinced us all to keep our mouths shut. But when I saw you guys come in, I just couldn't let the opportunity pass up, and ensured he couldn't escape."

"You bitch, you blocked my door," He seethed. "Hush Carlos, the adults are talking right now," I told him. "You can talk later when you beg for your life." I then looked at Hades, his cold silver eyes trying to cut right through me. "Now I hope we can come up with some way for all of us to get what we're owed." He and I then looked at Carlos who looked ready to piss his pants.

Later that night I sat at the table with a cigarette going over all the women's pay slips with Hades and one of the other men he had brought with him. Carlos was a very lucky man that he had a ton of cash undocumented in the safe. Unfortunately for him, it wasn't enough and now he has to go and get it with some Inferno chaperones. I was much faster working through the pay slips than them, and kept taking some of the ones from their stacks to quickly do the math on my note pad. I put my cigarette out and looked over each one, verifying everything was right. I then passed it to Hades. He began to count the cash while I leaned back in my chair, keeping one foot on the table for balance. I took a drink of my beer. More men came in and I wasn't surprised they were here.

He then handed me back the note pad, "Pass it out." He stood up to go talk to them. "Okay ladies, when I call your name come get it," I said and began to call their names, giving them what they were owed. When I finished Hades sat back down in front of me.

He held out some cash to me and I took it. I counted it, seeing it was more than what I was owed. "This is two more than I'm owed. What's the catch," I asked him with a raised eyebrow. "No catch," He told me. I laughed darkly, "There is always a catch, so what is it?" We then had a stare down, neither of us backing down. "The club will be under new management as of now, don't cause me any problems," He said while standing. I saluted, "Aye aye captain." I stood while tucking the cash into the back pocket of my shorts. I grabbed my leather jacket and put it on. Hades opened the door for me and I stepped into the freezing temperature. I began to walk while taking a cigarette out and lighting it.

A motorcycle pulled up beside me. It was Hades. "You're gonna freeze your ass off," He told me. I shrugged as I took a drag, "I'm used to the cold." "I'm gonna take you home," He told me. "I wasn't gonna go home," I told him. He raised an eyebrow, "And where would you be going this late at night?" "Marty's, they're twenty four hour and they make the best damn burgers," I told him. "Come on," He said. I put out my cigarette before slipping on to the back of his bike, my arms wrapping around his waist. Damn did it feel good be on the back of his bike. I took him to Marty's and we went in. "Hey Crimson," the woman who ran the place greeted. "Hey Bertha," I said as I made my way to my usual booth in the corner where I could see every entrance and exit.

"Why do they call you Crimson," He asked me. "Now it's because of my hair," I told him while running a hand through my hair that I pay good money to have dyed the color of blood. "Used to though it was because I was a hired mercenary. I had to go into temporary retirement when I got arrested and now I'm out on probation." "Clearly you weren't arrested for your profession," He said and I smirked, "Very good observation. You're right, I was arrested for being in possession of weapons that were illegal for a civilian to be in possession of." Bertha placed my usual order in front of me, "What can I get for you big guy?" He eyed my plate then look at her, "The same." She nodded and walked away.

"How long till your probation is up and you go back into business," He asked me. "Four months," I said while holding up four fingers. "What's your favorite weapon," He asked me curiously. I bit my lip as I thought about the array of tools I used for work. "It depends the job. I prefer getting up close and personal with my victims. I get off on the look of fear and realization that they're about to die when I look them in the eye before I end them. Just thinking of the memories gets me horny," I told him. Bertha brought his food, "Not in my diner Crimson." I smiled, "Of course not Bertha. Your good people, I'd never disrespect you like that." She smiled before going back to the kitchen. She was one of the few who knew my secret. In a way she was how jobs got a hold of me.

"So tell me, why the name Hades," I asked him curiously. He gave me a dark smirk that had me biting my lip, "Because I'm the King of the Underworld. I get off on torture and breaking bones." I smirked, "What's your body count?" "Seventeen," He answered. "You?" "Forty one," I told him. "You've got some catching up to do big guy." He chuckled, "I guess I do."

We finished eating and paid before I took him back to my apartment. Once inside he pinned me to the door, his lips on mine. He picked me up and I wrapped my legs around his waist. He knew exactly what to do when his tongue invaded my mouth. I moaned and buried my fingers in his hair. He moved me from the door to my bedroom. He laid me on the bed and began to undress me. He chuckled when he found the blades hidden in my knee high boots. When he had me stripped of my clothes, I laid there and watched him take the pistol out from the small of his back, and place it on the nightstand. I've never been so turned on by a man undressing before.

Once he was naked and his very large sheath was covered in a condom he didnt waist anytime entering me. I moaned and arched my back, my nails digging into his skin. He fucked like a savage, taking me to heights I've never been without the help of a drug. With him I didn't need any of that crap.

Afterwards we laid there. He had one arm behind his head, the other hand holding a cigarette. I laid with my head on his chest, smiling in satisfaction. The only things I knew in life was sex and death. At least I thought I knew what sex was before him. I sat up and ran a hand through my hair, which was a mess thanks to him. "Doesn't being a hired mercenary pay well," he asked me. "Yeah it does," I said while sitting up. "Then why do you live in a shit hole," He asked me. "Because the man who got me arrested fucked me big time. Took my money and beautiful condo, while the police took my weapons. I got the job at the club just so I could make some kind of living. Plus with Carlos taking a good chunk of my check I couldn't afford anything more decent," I told him while getting up. I felt sore in all the right places and I could feel his eyes watching me. "Plus to get back into the business, I need to save up and buy new toys once I'm no longer on parole." I took the cash out of my leather jacket and took out two grand then put the rest in. I put the two grand in my night stand. "I might be able to help get your toys back," He told me. I straddled his waist, "And what would that cost me?" His eyes trailed over my body, "I think I can find a good price for you. As long as if I'm ever in need of your services, I get a good price." I smirked as I lowered my lips to his, "I think I can agree to that." I then kissed his lips, enjoying the taste of us and tobacco on his tongue. I pulled away and took the cigarette from him, taking the final hit before putting it out in the ash tray on the nightstand. He flipped us, his hard cock pressing against my needy pussy, "If only I hadn't run out of condoms." I smirked, "Such a tragedy." "I'll make sure to bring more next time," he told me. "And what makes you think there will be a next time," I asked as a challenge. He chuckled coldly, "Because I'll be damned if I only fuck someone as good as you only once." He kissed me again before he got up to get dressed. He had a point, no way in hell was this going to be our only encounter.

Chapter 2

I got to the club and saw one of the bikers from last night running the place. I gave him a nod before going to get ready to start my shift. I had even noticed the club now had bouncers which deterred the patrons from trying to touch the dancers. They had the balls to touch me though as I passed them and I was ready to shove one of my knives down their throats. I went behind the bar and slammed my tray down in the kitchen, where the new manager was looking over the inventory. "Problem Crimson," He asked me. "Next fucker who touches my ass is getting a knife shoved up their dick," I told him. "You're not allowed to stab the patrons," He told me as he checked something off on his clipboard. "Can I stab them when they leave, they'll technically not be patrons then," I pointed out to him. "Sorry Princess, my dick isn't long enough to reach you through a visitation window at the jail," Hades said when he came in. "Now Princess is such a weak name, don't you think," I asked him with a smirk. He raised an eyebrow at me, "And what do you think is a better name?" I smirked, "Goddess, Empress, or Queen, take your pick." I then took my tray and left the kitchen. I jumped when he smacked my ass and I sent him a glare over my shoulder while he sent me a smirk over his. I rolled my eyes and went back to work.

Afterwards I was counting the register when Hades and the manager sat at the bar. "I don't think you've been introduced," Hades said. "This is Set, my VP." "The Greek God of the underworld and the Egyptian God of Chaos, nice," I told them with a small chuckle. Suddenly there were bullets flying and everyone hit the deck. Set and Hades jumped over the bar. It was quiet until the door was kicked down. I felt left out when Hades and Set popped up to return fire. So I sat on the bar between them and watched. I had grabbed a drink on my way up and enjoyed it as I watched the bodies drop. Firing stopped when everyone ran out of bullets.

"Your turn Crimson," Hades said. "I'll ensure this doesn't get back to you." I smiled with delight as I put down my drink. I took out my blades, "Now this is how you spend a Friday night." I stood leaped from the bar, flipping gracefully in the air, when I came down, both of my heels slammed into one of the unwelcomed visitors. They stood there frozen in fear as I stood on their buddy, my knives dancing between my fingers. "Oh come on now, don't tell me you boys are scared of me," I taunted. "W-We thought Crimson had died," One of them stuttered out. I smirked, "Well you're dead wrong." He was then the first the blades of my knives had killed. I almost laughed in joy as I took them out one by one. When I was done I turned to see Hades smirking at me. "Man you two have some fucked up relationship," Set said before taking a drink from a whiskey bottle. Hades chuckled, "Like yours and Julie's is any better." Set chuckled, "I guess you got a point there brother. I'll have Jakal come and clean this shit up." I pulled Hades to me and kissed him fiercely. "God it's been so long since I've had a rush like that," I said when we pulled away. He threw me over his shoulder and walked us to his bike. When he put me down, I was sitting on his bike, with him between my legs, kissing me. "How'd you feel if I was the one who arrested you for the night," He asked me when we pulled away for air. I bit my lip, "What would be my sentence?" "In my room without your clothes for me to use any way I want," He told me. I put my wrists together and held them up, "Then take me away sir, and have your wicked way with me."

He took me back to his club's compound and threw me over his shoulder. We went in and many gave us questioning looks, but neither of us said anything to them. When we got to his room he kicked the door shut and threw me on the bed. He pulled a pair of handcuffs from his nightstand and I smiled and let him keep me in his custody all night long.

Hades's POV

God this woman truly did put the hot in psychotic. She had a thirst for blood that rivaled my own. And the sex. Fuck the sex was amazing. One taste, and I was hooked. No way was I letting this woman go so easily. Shit wasn't supposed to go down tonight. I need to make sure her tracks were covered tonight or my addiction will end up behind bars. But god was she beautiful as she danced around the club taking out the remaining people. The fact she did it all in her six inch heeled boots was even hotter. I covered her when there was a knock on the door. I put on my boxers before opening the door. Trish was on the other side, wearing one of her tube tops and barely there shorts. She had been good for a casual fuck here and there, but she was no Crimson. "I have a problem I need you to help with," She said while looking up at me through her fake lashes. "Go find someone else," I told her. "I don't know if you heard but I came home with a real woman tonight, and she more than satisfied my needs." I let the door open more so she could see Crimson sleeping. "Y-You're letting her sleep in your bed," Trish asked, looking jealous. "You've never let a woman fall asleep after." I gave her a cold smirk, "Well maybe if any of you had rocked my world like she did, then you would've. Now if you don't excuse me, I'm gonna go join her." I shut the door in her face then turned to the bed. I stripped off my boxers and crawled into bed, pulling her body to me. God she fit so well, I thought before falling asleep.

I woke up and saw she was still asleep. I slipped out of the bed and threw on my jeans. I saw her knives were covered in dry blood so I took them downstairs to get them cleaned up. I sat at the bar polishing them when she came down the stairs dressed in last night's clothes. She smiled when she saw me polishing them. "Now there's a sexy sight," She said. I pulled her in for a kiss and she moaned softly, making me harden. "As much as I would love to have sex for breakfast, I need to go have my weekly meeting with my parole officer," She said. "So can you keep those in your room until I'm freed from my torture?" I nodded and stood, "Let me get dressed and I'll take you." "Such the gentleman," She said and I chuckled. I got dressed and went downstairs. I saw one of the pledges trying to catch her attention, but she casually ignored by playing a game on her phone. She then glared at him, "Call me Doll one more time, and I'm gonna shove my foot up your ass." He clearly hated the disrespect she gave him, and I could see he wanted to put her in her place. Little did he know, she already was. I wrapped an arm around her waist, "Come on, don't want you to be late." She looked up at me with a smile, and I lead her out of the compound.

When we got to where she was supposed to meet her parole officer she kissed me once she got off my biker. I gave her my number, telling her to text me when she was done. I didn't pull out until she was inside and I went to see the damage done to the club. Set and Jakal were there already. Set smirked, "Rumors true, she slept in your bed?" I nodded, "And I right next to her." Jakal whistled, "Damn she must be special if she got that kind of honor." Set chuckled, "When you meet her, you'll understand."

We then became serious, "So who are the fucks that thought they could come in and shoot up my club?" "Raging Bull," Set answered. "Wonderful, a bunch of pussies that cant find themselves out of a wet paper sack," I said. Raging Bull were a bunch of idiots who did shit out if impulse. They were trying to make a name for themselves and in reality the only name they have for themselves is that they're stupid idiots. "What are we gonna do," Jakal asked me. "They'll come after us for killing their men."

"We makes sure they get the message and never try to fuck with us again," I told them. "I want this shit over before Valentine's Day gets here." Which was in February but Christmas was just a couple weeks away and then we have New Years and none of us would want to deal with this shit during that time.

When she sent me a text telling me she was ready I went and picked her up. On the way to pick her up it began to snow. A blizzard was forecasted to hit us hard. The compound was well prepared of that happening but was she? I took her back to her place and shook the snow out of my hair, "What are you gonna do during the blizzard?" "Hunker down and hope for the best. I also pray it doesnt bust my sliding doors like it did last year when it couldn't handle the wait of the snow that piled against it," she told me. I eyed the sliding doors that lead to her balcony. They didn't seem all that sturdy.

"Come stay at the compound," I told her. "We have more than enough supplies." She smirked, "What about condoms?" I pulled her to me, "That I will have to stock up on. If you want to then come on before the snow traps us here." She nodded and went to her room. She packed a back pack of clothes and such before we left. The snow fell lightly still by the time we got back. I put my bike in the garage along with everyone elses before taking her inside.

Everyone was getting ready for it and I took her upstairs to my room. "I'm gonna go to the store, text me and let me know if you need anything," I told her. She nodded and I left. Set was at the bottom of the stairs with a list given to him from his wife. We went to my truck that had snow tires on it and left. "I cant believe you're letting her stay during the Blizzard," he said with a smirk. "She didnt have much thanks to Carlos, plus fucking is a great way to pass the time," I told him with a shrug. At the store I stocked up on condoms while Set got what his wife needed. I got a simple text from Crimson asking for a box of hot chocolate and mini marshmallows. I didn't peg her for the type that took marshmallows in her hot chocolate, I figured she was the black coffee type of woman. Interesting.

I got back to the compound and found her lounging on my bed, playing a game on her phone. She laughed at the bag of condoms in one hand and the hot chocolate and marshmallows in the other. "Had to make sure we were prepared," I told her. "So what do you all usually do when blizzards hit around here," she asked curiously. "Well some fuck a lot, we play our instruments, we drink, and try to stay warm," I told her. She smiled, "Sounds like fun."

There was a knock on the door and I opened it. On the other side was Jullie with her bright pink clipboard, that had her inventory lists. "Everyone is accounted for at all the chapters that's gonna get hit and all the supplies are accounted for," she told me and I took the lists with a nod. "Thanks," I said she then eyed Crimson on the bed. She gave me a knowing smile and walked away. I shook my head and shut the door. I sat on the bed and grabbed my reading glasses to look over them. I heard a soft giggle then heard the snapping of a picture. I looked over at her and she gave me a smile, "You look sexy in glasses." I chuckled and went back to looking at the forms. When I confirmed everything was in order and looked right, I put them on my dresser.

"So tell me," She said putting her phone down. "I dont know about biker politics, but I do know you have different meanings when it comes to relationships and things like that. If we keep spending time together like we have, what will I be considered when it pertains to you?" "Well you'll be seen as my woman, and if you slept with another brother or pledge then it will be seen as you cheating on me, and it would be the same if I slept with another woman," I explained to her. "You will receive some hatred from many of the women I once had sex with because with you I am breaking damn near every rule I've ever put in place for myself." She giggled softly, "And what were those rules." "One, never let a woman I've had sex with fall asleep in my bed or I in her bed," I told her. "Two, never fuck her more than once in the same week. Three, never let a woman ride on the back of my bike. Four, let the woman know her place is far below me. Five, never fall in love."

She smirked, "So I've slept in your bed, we've had sex more than once this week, and I've ridden on the back of your bike a few time. Just so we're clear, where is my place?" It was a challenge, and damn was it a fun one. "Where do you want that place to be," I asked her, challenging her back. "The only time I want to be above, or under you, is when we're having sex. I dont neccesarily want to be by your side, but around the same level would be nice," she said. "Only when it comes to respect though, after all it's your club and you're its leader so all the power goes to you. And I'm glad your fifth rule is something we can both agree on. I dont do love."

She had a dark look in her eyes as she finished. She was a mercenary, it was a no brainer why she didn't do love. I was a biker who did illegal shit, it was a no brainer why I didnt do it either. Now that we got that settled, it was time to enjoy ourselves during this blizzard.

Chapter 3

In the middle of the night the blizzard knocked out the power, and the heater. "Fuck its cold," Hades grumbled as he got up to throw on a pair of sweat pants. I could hear others up and griping about the cold, and dragging what sounded like their mattresses downstairs since there was a large fireplace in the common room. "Come on Crimson, we're gonna go downstairs," he muttered. I threw on his shirt and my underwear, not bothered by the cold. He and one other took his mattress downstairs while others were getting the fire started. Everyone was bundled up and I got weird looks as I stood on the wooden wooden floor in my underwear and Hades shirt. They'll be stripping it all off once it got hot in here anyways. Plus the cold was something I was used too.

I laid on Hades's mattress while he was busy. I was starting to drift back to sleep when he came over and looked down at me with a raised eyebrow. "You're gonna get sick," he said. I yawned, "It feels nice in here." He shook his head and stripped off the sweatshirt he threw on before coming down. He cursed softly before crawling into bed and threw the covers over us. He pulled me to him, making me lay on top of him for the most part. I shifted till I was comfortable before falling back to sleep.

I woke up later to the sun streaming in and some whispers. "They'll kill you if you wake them up," I heard Set whisper harshly. "They're the last ones asleep and their food will get cold and there isn't really any way to reheat it," a woman said. That had me sitting up to my knees, careful of the big guy beneath me. One of my legs was between his and the last thing I wanted to do was injure his manhood.

I yawned and got up as Hades went to grab me, "Come on big guy, breakfast." He grumbled some curses about the cold and how it was cruel to leave him like that. I sat down and waited for him to drag his ass out of bed. He threw on his sweatshirt and sat down silently. The food was freshly cooked, most likely having a gas stove to be able to cook it. Hades got up and went upstairs before coming down with my box of hot chocolate and some marshmallows. He made us each a cup then sat back down.

No powers means no coffee maker but hot water can be boiled on the stove since they made sure to have the faucets drip to keep the pipes from freezing so they'd have running water. If I was more awake I would've laughed at the thought of big and scary drinking hot chocolate with marshmallows. After breakfast we all washed out dishes then huddled in the common room. When a lot of us thawed out and became awake they broke out the instruments. Even Hades brought a guitar. The voice he had when he sang wasn't fair, for a man so hard and tough to have.

When they began to play Picture by Kid Rock and Sheryl Crow the women joined on Sheryl's parts, and I did too. Hades met my eyes as I sang along, a small smile on his lips and shock in his eyes. For hours everyone played, sang, and danced, enjoying the chance to just kick back while the storm raged on outside. Later that night Hades heated up water for his bathtub the old fashioned way, by boiling water on the stove in a large pot. I put a battery powered lantern in there so we could see. We stripped and got in, my back against his chest. It was our only way of getting privacy while also staying warm.

"Where'd you learn to fight like that," He asked me. "You wouldn't believe me if I told you," I said before lighting a cigarette. I held it up so he could take a hit, "Try me." I sighed, feeling weird since no one had ever asked me that before. "When I was an infant I was dropped off at some run down orphanage. A man came in a week or so later and adopted me. I was taken care of by a woman named Sylvia who was far from the motherly type. Once I turned ten I was thrust in with the other kids who had been adopted, and were being trained to become ruthless mercenaries. You bikers have your clubs, while we mercenaries have our guilds. I was the only girl that had been adopted to become a killer. Even being trained to use my beauty as a weapon. The Guild Master saw great potential in me and personally took me under his wing and ensured I received the best training money could buy. Part of that training was to be able to withstand the elements, hence why the cold doesn't bother me. I've traveled all over the world as a kid learning how to kill and torture, from old school to new school. I was thirteen when I took my first kill." "Who was it," He asked with curiosity, not judgement. "My biological parents," I told him before I took a drag of the cigarette. I blew out the smoke with a sigh, "It was a test to see if I was ready to start making money to start paying off my debt for the Guild Master saving me from the shit hole he found me." I gave a dark laugh, "I had no problem killing them, because I blamed them for the hell I had gone through. If they had kept me, I would've had a normal childhood." I put the cigarette out and leaned my head against his shoulder, "Now your turn, how did you end up joining Inferno?"

"Growing up my dad had been in this gang. They had more fucked up morals than we do here. They had no honor and did shit that makes my blood boil every time I think about it. My mom hated me because my dad stopped loving her when her body didn't go back to normal after she had me. She became a heart broken drunk who beat on me all the time when I became about four or five. When I was fourteen I had enough and I fucking ran, not once looking back. I lived on the road, going wherever the wind took me. I earned money in underground fights, and slept wherever looked comfortable. I was asleep in Central park a few blocks from here at the age of sixteen when Hoss, our previous President, found me. He gave me a choice, become a man or stay bein' a rat. Tired of bein' a rat, I decided to become a man. Shortly after I was patched in, I got a call from a cop, telling me my parents needed to be bailed out. I rode my bike down there, not because I wanted to bail them out, but because I wanted them to take a good hard look at the man I had become. God it felt good seeing the fear in my mother's eyes when she saw me. My dad was too hungover to even fuckin' notice. I told the cop they could rot for all I cared, then I left."

We both had fucked up childhoods, that made us into who we were today. "What's one thing you've always wanted as a child, even until this day," He asked me next. I scoffed, "God this is probably gonna sound stupid." He kissed my head, "That's okay. It's just us." I sighed, "I've always wanted a charm bracelet. Even when I was free, I never mustered up the balls to buy one, because I felt the charms should have meaning, like I had seen many girls talk about when I passed by them in malls and such." I then tilted my head up to look at him, "What about you?" "A Celtic cross necklace," He answered. "I'm not a religious person but I always admired the way they looked." We then became silent, simply enjoying the comfort only we could offer each other. We were fucked up beyond belief, not meant for those who walk in the light of day care free. Blood, pain, and death was our first nature, while surviving was our second. It was why we clicked so well and had the comfort we did, because we knew we'd never run into someone who understands, like we understand each other. When the water began to become cold we quickly dried off and dressed before going downstairs. Some were on their beds having sex, some played poker, some were drinking. We crawled under the covers, something different settling between us when we looked each other in the eyes. I felt the shift in me then, the coldness I knew so well. I saw something similar creep into his eyes as well. That night we fell asleep with our backs facing each other.

Chapter 4

Christmas, what a wonderful time of year to be reminded of all the things I'm not. Things like cheerful, nice, and anything else involving the word good. I hated the lights, the decorations, and the music. The only good thing that Christmas brought around were some really good cookies. I especially loved the peanut butter ones with the Hershey kiss in the center that Set's wife had made for me. Set has been the only one I've seen on a day to day basis.

Since that night Hades and I got deep we became really shallow. During the blizzard we didn't really interact unless it was to have sex somewhere. When it was cleared enough for me to get home, I left, leaving only a simple text, Went home. I had left so early no one was awake yet meaning I walked. It was fine with me, I didn't really care.

After that I only saw Hades in passing, like when he was at the club talking with Set, or riding past on his bike. My heart clenched and my pussy ached everytime I saw him, and I didn't understand it. I don't even know why I felt the need to buy Hades a stupid Christmas present. I didn't have the balls to give it to him personally so I used my skills in breaking and entering to sneak through his bedroom window and put it on his pillow last night when he was busy fucking another woman.

It hurt knowing he was fucking another woman, but it made me smug when I realized he hadn't fucked a single one in his bed since we fucked. He keeps his rules strictly in place with them and I couldn't help but feel happy about that. It was fucking stupid.

Plus I'm no better. I've let guys take me home for a casual fuck but none of them were as good as him. I haven't even had an orgasm since the last time we fucked a couple weeks ago. Was this Karma for taking those lives in the club? Nah, Karma stopped trying to get me since I was a kid.

I walked into the club and saw Hades and Set having a beer at one of the tables. The light caught a shine on the Celtic cross necklace he wore around his neck and I felt something weird in my chest. Ugh fuck this shit, I thought as I went to go clock in. Tonight was to be a very busy night, like every Christmas eve. Tonight the club will be filled with men who realized they have no one to spend Christmas here so they come to blow the money they would've spent on presents, on dances from the women.

Tonight the strippers would be dancing to Christmas music while wearing skimpy Christmas outfits. Set tried to get me to wear an outfit similar to what the girls in that movie Mean Girls wear during their performance. I told him if he suggested it again he and his wife will never be able to have kids. To try and seem a little bit festive I got a cropped tank top with red glitter writing saying Always on the Naughty List. That was as far as I was gonna get.

Tonight after the club closed there was gonna be a small Christmas party with the staff and I planned on slipping out.

When the club opened, for once Hades stayed. Watching me. I smiled the fake smile I mastered years ago as I made my way through the club. The tips were heavier than normal tonight which was always a plus in my opinion. I counted the register as everyone began to gather. The woman talked and laughed while the guys cracked one a cold one. The sooner I was out of here the better.

I slipped out the back and began to walk home when a bike pulled up next to me. It was Hades. "Get on Crimson," He said. I looked him over, my eyes landing on the necklace before going to his eyes. I took a long drag from my cigarette then flicked off the ashes. "Why should I," I asked him after a moment. "Because I'm not in the mood to spend Christmas alone," He told me. I scoffed, "You've got an entire club to spend it with." "They're all with their families," he lied. I smirked, "I bet your little fuck buddy is available if you call her." His jaw clenched and he parked his bike, getting off of it. "I tried to rid myself of the taste of you," he told me. "Tried to find something better, and I know damn well you did too." I nodded, "I ain't gonna lie about that, I tried and I failed."

"Then let's cut the crap," he told me. "I need a good fuck and so do you." I shook my head, "You dont fucking get it. I let you close! I, the heartless Crimson, who can kill a man before breakfast, let you close. Let you know my fucked up past and a hidden desire I have." Was I angry at him? At myself? Fuck if I knew.

"I cant let shit like that happen, especially when I come out of retirement," I told him. "Yet I want to tell you shit because I know you're the only one on this God damn planet who understands me. I want to let you close, but if I do that you'll get killed!" There is was all out in the open. I liked telling him what I did. I wanted to tell him more. I wanted him to know the woman beneath the blood and gore. Just like I want to know the man beneath it all as well. He was then kissing me, his tongue invading my mouth. I dropped my cigarette in the snow and wrapped my arms around him. He pulled away and rested his forehead against mine. "Every woman I fucked I couldn't even get hard for without thinking of you. I hoped it would rid myself of the memories of how good it was, but I just kept comparing them. I want someone who I want to break every damn rule I have and not give a fuck about the consequences. I want to want to lay in bed afterwards with her asleep beside me while I smoke a cigarette after giving her the fucking of a life time. I want her to ride on the back of my bike or in the passenger seat of my truck, teasing me to the point I find a private road and fuck her brains out. I want to wake up beside her knowing she wont see me as a fucking monster or look at me with pity. And damn it all to hell Crimson, that's you. I'm not saying I love you, but I am saying I want you. We're two fucked up people who have never had an ounce of normalcy in their lives and why should our relationship be any different?"

"I could get you killed, have a target slapped on to your back with a sign above your head screaming, here I am! What part of that do you not get," I asked him. "And what point of, I dont give a fuck, dont you understand? I already have a target on my back, comes with the territory of being President," He told me. I pulled away to run a hand through my hair. "Fuck," I said. I've never called someone mine. Never even thought of it. Until him. "Come on Crimson, we only live once," He told me.

I turned on my heel to face him, "Fine, but I'm going to train you to be able to fight if any mercenaries want to use you to get to me." I then pulled him to me, kissing him as if I had been starving. When he pulled away, he took my hand and lead me over to his bike. We got back to my apartment and he pinned me to the door. We didn't waist any time going to the bedroom, and just took each other in front of my front door. We fucked for hours, our bodies having missed each other more than our minds had wanted to express.

We laid on the floor, my body on his, sticky with sweat. We were both panting and tired. I was beginning to have trouble keeping my eyes open. "Come on Crimson, let's get to the bed," He said softly. I got up, my legs feeling like jelly. He smirked and scooped me up, carrying me to the bed. He laid me down and crawled under the covers with me. He pulled me to him and I snuggled into his chest before letting sleep take me away.

Chapter 5

I woke up the next morning to the smell of bacon being fried and Hades not being in bed. I sat up and stretched then a small square box sitting on my nightstand with a tag that had my name on it. I picked it up and looked down at my first ever Christmas present. I gently opened the wrapping paper then the lid of the box. Inside was a silver charm bracelet. There was a motorcycle, a pistol, a rose, a knife, a skull, and a padlock. I ran my hand over it, smiling softly. I put on then slipped on Hades shirt before leaving the room. He stood at the stove so I wrapped my arms around his waist from behind. "I love it, thank you," I told him. He rested a hand on mine, not saying anything. We stayed like that until he finished cooking before going over to the couch to eat while watching Die Hard, the only Christmas movie I liked. Some argue it's not, a Christmas movie, but to me it is and those who say differently can suck it.

After we ate, we just put our dishes on the coffee table and got comfortable. "So what do you usually do for Christmas," I asked him curiously. "Fuck a willing woman or get drunk," He answered. "You?"

I shrugged, "Get drunk, go kill someone if I had been hired, spend the day cleaning every weapon I had, threaten Christmas carolers, and other things along those lines."

"And what did you do when you were part of the guild," He asked me. "Some of the kids would sneak out to go play in the snow while I stayed inside. One of the older kids would snitch on them and then I was forced to watch the guildmaster beat them for not following the rules. One year, when we were fifteenish we drugged the guildmaster and went out to get tattoos," I sighed, "Unfortunately he made us go through the hell of getting that tattoo removal crap. That shit hurt more than getting it. He thought it was a good test of our pain tolerance and how long we could handle it. I was smart though and got a small one on my wrist while some had bigger. He didn't want us to have them so we couldn't have any identifying markers."

"What did you get," He asked curiously. "A pink tulip," I told him. "I think about it now and it seems so stupid. A hardened killer with a girly tulip tattoo. Yet I had loved it for the small amount of time I had it." "Its not stupid," he told me. "I can even take you to get another one if you want."

I looked at him and I could tell he was serious. "So what is something that you've wanted that you feel its stupid?" "To ride a roller coaster," He admitted. "Growing up there was always this carnival I wanted to go too and ride the rides but I was never allowed. When I left and was surviving on the streets, having to save every penny. When I joined Inferno I never went because I didn't want the others to look down on me for doing something childish."

I smiled, "I dont see that as stupid. I think it sounds like a good time. You can use taking me as an excuse so it doesnt hurt your ego. Instead you'll be seen as someone taking care of their woman." He chuckled, "I guess I could." "Plus I've never been either. I've been zip lining in the Amazon though, but I doubt that's the same thing."

"The Amazon," He asked with a raised eyebrow. "One of the men the guildmaster hired lived in a large tree house in the Amazon. The zip line went straight through the forest. It was a lot of fun," I explained to him. He chuckled, "Interesting."

We then fell silent again, just watching the movie, but neither paying attention to it. When it ended I got up and stretched. His eyes followed the hemline of his shirt, watching it reveal more and more. I smirked at him and put my arms down, causing the shirt to recover me. He looked disappointed and I laughed at him.

He then pulled me towards him, kissing me like his life depended on it. Suddenly his phone rang, breaking our kiss. He grabbed my ass, keeping me close, as he reached over for his phone. "What," he said when he answered it. He then got to his feet, "I'm on my way."

He hung up, "The compound is under attack." We quickly got dressed, and he stopped me when he saw me pull a thing of throwing knives out of my drawer. "No, you're not getting mixed up with this," he told me. "Police could end up getting mixed in, and I dont need you getting arrested." "But I want to help," I argued. He pulled me to him, kissing me. "Please my Persephone," He whispered against my lips and it made my knees weak. I looked into his eyes and saw the true fear of something happening to me in his eyes. It made my heart flutter. I nodded, "For you I will stay out of it. But if you get hurt, I'm going to go hunting." He kissed me again before leaving and I sighed, locking the door.

I decided to take a shower while I waited for him to either come back or for him to call me. I had just stepped out and wrapped a towel around me when there was a loud bang on my front door. I took down my shower curtain when there was another bang and it was obvious someone was trying to get in. At the sound of the third bang, I had the shower curtain off and my towel pinned in place. I stepped into my bedroom when I heard the door bang against the wall as whoever it was came into the apartment.

My bedroom door was then kicked in and I was ready for them. There were ten of them. "Hey boss, we got her. Hades has chosen a nice piece of ass for himself," One said, coming in while on the phone. He then put his phone on speaker, "Do what I want or your girl gets it?"

"You okay Crimson," I heard Hades said, meaning the phone was on speaker on both sides. "I have ten men in my room, and I'm in my towel," I told him. "Whatever you do, make sure it doesn't fall off, I'd hate for them to get a view of something so beautiful before they die," He told me. I smirked, "Start counting, I wanna see how long this takes." "One..." He began.

"What kind of shit is this," Someone on the other end said. "I bet fifty she gets them all by the count of twenty," I heard Set say in the background. I had begun using the shower curtain as a spear, fighting with it with ease. I couldn't help the smile I had as I took them out.

"Fifteen..."Hades said as the last fell to the floor. I picked up the phone, "That's a new record. I've never killed ten men before with a shower curtain rod. Thank you sir for having your men knock my door down and giving me the chance to see how fun it is. Of course it's not as fun using my knives, but it was entertaining." I still had my smile but my tone dropped to something darkly and deadly. "Now you listen here, you have ruined my Christmas, by dragging my man away from my bed, and by making me get blood all over one of my good towels. Now I want you to follow my instructions closely. I want you to get your goons to get out of Inferno territory, or I will be painting the walls of your compound Crimson." I then hung up and dialed the police.

I stood outside by my parole officer's car, discussing what happened. "Do you know why they broke down your door," He asked him. "I'm dating the Inferno's President," I told him. "Word on the street is they're trying to start a war, and wanted to target me." He sighed, "Really Vixen? He'll get your ass locked up quicker than you can blink." I shook my head, "MCs aren't like gangs Mickey. They keep their women away from the illegal things. You can't tell me I wasn't in my right here when I took them out." He nodded with a sigh, "That you were. I have never seen, killed ten men with a shower curtain rod in self defense, written in a police report before. That's surely a first."

A bike pulled out and Hades got off of it. His eyes trailed over me, and I saw rage and worry in them. "She isn't going to get arrested is she," He asked Mickey. Mickey studied Hades, seeing the same genuine worry I did. He shook his head, "They kicked her front door and bedroom door down trying to get her. Vixen was well within her right." Hades nodded as he took off his leather jacket and draped it around my shoulders. I pulled it closer to me, enjoying the scent of his cologne. "I'll let you go to get warm," Mickey told me. "Am I allowed back into my apartment," I asked him. He shook his head, "Unfortunately not. They're still processing the crime scene." I nodded and I noticed Hades's jaw was clenched. I took his hand, "Come on big guy. Let's go to the compound."

I had to sit on his bike side saddle because of the towel, and it was annoying. I can honestly say this is a first for me. We get to the compound and I saw several bullet holes in the common room, but no blood. Many were already patching up the damages. In his room I traded his jacket and towel for one of his shirts. "They're going to be processing the crime scene for a while, plus you have to wait for the damages done to your apartment before you can get any of your clothes," He told me. "I think you left a pair of your shorts and a shirt here though, so tomorrow we can go out and buy you clothes." "On the day after Christmas," I asked him. "And I thought I was insane." I plopped on his bed, "Plus my debit card and cash are in my apartment."

He smirked, "I know." I shook my head, "You have spent enough on me." "That's just a fucking bracelet Crimson," He told me. "That is sterling silver with real gold on the rims of the motorcycle, the grip of the knife and pistol, and there is also real diamonds in the eyes of the skull," I pointed out to him. "That's a lot of money." He pulled me to him, "And you're my girl. I want to spend that and more on you, and right now you don't have much choice but to let me or I'm gonna have to rip every guy's eyes out of their heads for looking at you if you were to only walk around in that towel or my shirt." I smirked and crossed my arms, pushing my breasts up, drawing his eyes to them, then back to mine.

"You didn't seem to mind during that time we got snowed in," I told him. "I did, but you weren't mine then and I had no right. Now though, it's another story," He countered. I sighed and laid back, "Okay fine." He smiled and came over, putting a hand on either side of my head as he leaned down. "Now that's more like it." He kissed me like a savage and I fucking loved it. It may have been a bloody Christmas like many others I have, but at least this year I truly did enjoy my Christmas.

Chapter 6

I sat at the food court eating my burger while keeping all of my grumblings about how I hated Hades buying me things, to myself. He bought me a whole new wardrobe! Of course they were things I dont think I would have ever bought for myself if it was just me. A lot of the things were girly and feminine. Things deep down, I have always wanted. God what was this man doing to me? I'm a ruthless killer who wears six inch heels most women would break their neck wearing and leather, not floral print sundresses. Although the pink and white one I got was super cute.

We were enjoying our food when I got the feeling we were being watched. I casually looked around. "Back by the chinese," Hades said under his breath when I noticed them. My blood ran cold as I took a drink from my soda. "They're mercenaries from my guild," I whispered. "Then I suggest we leave and see what they want," he said and I nodded. We finished our food and threw it away. Hades grabbed my bags and we left.

In the parking lot we met them at Hades's car. "We need to talk Vixen," Croft said softly. He was a man who specialized in ancient torture techniques. Nothing was impossible for him to extract from someone. "About," I asked him. "Our Master," Zenith answered. Zenith was a poisons expert. He loved making poisons that were impossible to cure. "He was killed by seated blades, much like the special ones you carry," Croft told me. I scoffed, "Please if I had killed him you'd know. Plus I haven't had those blades since I was arrested a while back. Check with Sible, after all he was the reason I was arrested in the first place. My weapons were confiscated and my condo taken."

"We can't ask him, he's dead," Croft told me. I snapped a finger, "Damn and I was hoping for my revenge. I didn't off him either, I'm on probation for a couple more months." I then gestured to Hades, "Plus he's been keeping me very busy." "And you two are interfering with our day. We have an appointment to get to in thirty so if those are all the questions you have for my woman, I suggest you get out of town," he told them coldly. The way he threatened them and called me his had me wanting to jump his bones. I'm not against taking him here in the parking garage, but he wouldn't want someone to see what was for his eyes only. I didn't mind having a possessive man, I was just as bad. It's not like it was the kind where he kept me from talking to the male species, he's just threatening those he sees as a threat. I would do the same.

Croft nodded, "Message understood by us." He then looked me in the eye, "Ice on the other hand is convinced it was you. He's got an eye on you Crimson." Then they were gone.

Once in the car Hades looked at me, "Who's Ice?" "A bastard who has always hated me. He was always jealous about the time the Master put into grooming me to be the perfect mercenary. He was also his biological son," I told him. "He is called Ice because he enjoys watching his victims slowly freeze to death."

"And the two who I met today," he asked. "Croft, who was the bigger of the two, and Zenith. Croft is a torture expert while Zenith is an expert in poisons," I told him. He nodded and started the car. "So what appointment do we have to make," I asked him curiously. "You have an appointment with our tattoo artist," he told me. My eyes lit up, and I couldn't help my smile.

We pulled up to the tattoo shop and he opened the door for me. A man with a white beard and bald head was behind the counter. "This the woman I've heard so much about," He asked Hades. Hades nodded, "This is my woman, Crimson. She will get to be one of the few people you get to do the water color style you enjoy so much on." He held his hand out to me, "I'm Ink. As you can tell it's for obvious reasons." I shook his hand, "It's nice to meet you Ink." "So what are you getting today," he asked me. I turned to Hades, "So what is it that you brought me here to get?" He pulled out a paper from his back pocket and unfolded it before handing it to Ink. Ink looked it over before nodding, "This is completely doable."

Neither let me see it though and Hades decided to blind fold me during the whole process. The guys talked the entire time while I sat there with the blindfold on, simply listening to them.

Hades's POV

I found it funny seeing her excitement as she sat during the whole tattoo process getting the three pink tulips that went from wrist to elbow on the underside of her right arm. She was annoyed by the blindfold but she'll get over it. When she saw it her smile was worth everything. It wasn't one brought on by dark things, but instead it was brought on by something good. I wanted to make that smile last as long as possible.

After leaving the parlor, I took her to get her nails done before taking her back to the compound. She collapsed onto the bed, on her stomach, once it was all put away, "That was so exhausting." I chuckled at her, "You truly aren't a woman who enjoys a shopping spree." "For weapons I am," she corrected. I laid on top of her so I covered her, my face in the crook of her neck.

She sighed softly. "Thank you for the tattoo," she whispered. "I thought my Persephone deserved her flowers," I told her softly. I placed a kiss on her neck. The moment was broken when someone knocked on the door. I sighed and got up. I found Set on the other side holding a stack of paper work that had to get done. Set smirked, "There's no getting out of it tonight." I sighed and looked back at Crimson. She gave me a teasing smile, "Have fun. I'm sure I can find something to occupy my time with." I went over and gave her a kiss before leaving to follow Set to my office inside of Church.

"Enjoy yourself," Set asked curiously. I nodded, "We had a slight hiccup when two of her old guild members approached us at the mall. Apparently their master was killed and someone named Ice is convinced she did it because the blades used were a lot like the ones she used to use. Only problem is she doesnt have her weapons. Not since the police confiscated them at least. She told them to go ask the person who got her arrested, but they can't do that because he was killed as well."

"I think someone is trying to set her up," Set said. I nodded in agreement, "My thoughts exactly." "So what are you going to do," He asked me. I sighed, "I dont know. Bikers I can face, but if they're just as good as her, then I'm fucked when it comes to protecting her." "So ask her to teach you," Set said simply. "I dont know," I said with a shake of my head.

"Someone is targeting your old lady, and they'll target you to get to her," he told me. "Old lady," I asked him. Since when, I thought. He chuckled, That's what we see her as. Just waitin' on you to declare her."

I shook my head, "I don't know about that." "What makes you say that," he asked me. "She's only stuck in this damn city because of her probation. Once it's over shes gonna be able to do what she's good at, and go wherever she wants," I explained to him. "I dont see her staying here once her probation is over." "And if she leaves," he asked me.

I sighed, "I'll understand. She loves to live dangerously. More dangerously than either of us dare too. Her staying and being with me will keep her from that." "Did you ever ask if she wanted that kind of life," Set asked me. "That's all she knows Hades. Maybe, just maybe, she might actually want something different. Something you can give her. No one else could ever accept her for who she is the way you do."

I nodded, knowing he was right. Vixen was a special woman that no normal man could handle. Thankfully I'm not normal.

Chapter 7

<hr>

I was sitting on the couch in the common room while Hades was in a meeting in Church. Julie came over to me excitedly. "Let's go shopping for our New Year party dresses," she said excitedly. The party Caged Beasts was planning, was going to be the party of the century. At least that's what Julie claims. I stood up, "That sounds like a great idea."

I went upstairs to get changed. I put on the cute white and pink floral dress that had three quarter sleeves and stopped above my knees. I paired the dress with black tights and black heeled boots. I put on a black thin choker and did simple make up. I curled my hair before going downstairs. Hades and Set were just coming inside as we were getting ready to leave. "And where do you think you two are going," Set asked while crossing his arms.

"Shopping," Julie told him with a smile. "We need our dresses for the party." "Without us," Hades asked me with a raised eyebrow. I smirked, "That was the plan." He chuckled darkly, "And let you spend your own money? I don't think so."

Set nodded, "I agree. We're coming along." Julie and I shared a look then sighed in unison. I then smiled and took Hades's hand. Hades lead us out to his truck and opened the door for me. The entire drive to the mall, Julie and Set talked, never running out of things to talk about while Hades and I simply held hands as he drove.

We had turned a corner when a large truck shot out to block the road. Hades slammed the breaks and we were only inches from slamming into it. I saw Fallyn at the wheel and I knew what was about to happen. "Come on Crimson. We just need to talk," Fallyn said once he got out of the truck. He then held up a remote, "If you don't I'm just gonna blow you all sky high." I turned to Hades and gave him a kiss, before slipping from the truck quickly. Tranquilizer darts hit the three of them before I could shut the door. My heart clenched as I shut the door. I put my hands on my head as Fallyn came over and frisked me.

"Just being careful," He said as he gestured for me to go to the truck. Once in the truck I got comfortable before the expected prick of the needle came and darkness took me.

I woke up laying in my old bed at the Guild house. I groaned in stretched and saw the sky was lightening meaning it was the next day. I got up and put my shoes on. I opened the door and saw that although my room was the same, the house was differently entirely. I found the stairs and went down them. I stopped when I saw everyone in the living room. "Why was I brought here," I asked them.

"To have Master's will read," Ice said, his arms crossed. "So I take it you guys found his killer," I asked while leaning in the doorway. Zenith nodded, "Yeah. He was killed by Corrine, who had also killed Sible. Apparently her and Sible were in it together to get you arrested." He dropped a file down filled with messages the two had shared. "Where is she now," I asked as I looked through.

"We don't know, but she is still after you," Zenith told me. I stiffened, "And you left my man and friends there, unconscious, for her to find?!"

"We had our fledglings watching them until a few of those bikers came and picked them up," Croft told me. "Let's hurry up and read the damn will so I can get back," I told them.

Lariat, our guild's lawyer, opened his brief case and pulled out the papers. He read off various amounts of money and who it goes too. It was the last part that had my stomach clenching to the point I want to hurl. "To Vixen Holly, I leave my guild, weapons, jewels, and fourty billion dollars."

I stumbled a step back, "I don't want the guild. I'm still on probabtion." Ice held up some forms, "Not anymore you're not. I had a feeling the old man would give the guild to you so I made arrangements." I was shocked to see he wasn't infuriated that I was given the guild. Then again, I could understand why. None of us wanted to have the guild. It was filled with horrible memories.

I took the forms from him and read he had gotten it lifted. That was the only good thing to come from this. I then thought of Hades. I had begun thinking of having a good life, one where I was no longer killing unless I had too. "So what do we do Mistress," Croft asked me. "You guys have to understand, I did something no mercenary should ever do. I made ties. Ties I refuse to cut. I'm happy for once, and that happiness isn't brought on by death or pain. It's brought on because I'm in love." I ran a hand through my hair as realization slammed into me. I loved Hades. And it had been so easy to say I did.

They continued to stare at me. "You can have those ties Crimson. You can change us for the better," Ice told me. "Hell we would all like to have ties to someone." Zenith nodded, "We would. Go talk this over with him. We aren't far from your home." I looked out the window and realized he was right. We were in a mansion just a few blocks away from the compound.

I took my copy of the will and left. I walked as I tried to get my thoughts straight. I was shocked to see the bikes were gone when I got there. I walked in and saw Julie sitting on the couch in the common room, her mascara running. "Crimson!" She said hoping over the couch and hugged me so tightly the air left my lungs. I returned her hug, the papers crinkling in my hand. She then let me go and pulled her phone out.

"Set, Crimson is here," She said in a rush. She passed the phone over to me, "Where the fuck have you been?" Set snapped.

"Its a long story. One I need to talk to Hades about." I then hung up and handed her the phone. I went upstairs and stripped off my clothes. I left the papers on the bathroom counter and began to fill the tub with hot water and bubbles. I tied my hair up and got in.

"Persephone," I heard Hades say when he came into the room. "In here," I told him. He came in and I turned to face him. He had dark circles under his eyes, caused by my disappearance. I gestured to the papers, "They took me so they could have the will our Master left behind."

He picked them up and read them both. His eye brows shot up as he read the will. He whistled, "That's a lot of money." I nodded, "Yeah it is." He folded them up and left the on the counter, "Now that you're a free woman, what do you plan to do?"

I shook my head, "I'm not a free woman, Hades. I'm your woman." I got out and wrapped a towel around myself, "I wanted to talk to you about it because whatever I choose, affects us both. I love you and I'm not going to just think of myself anymore."

"W-What did you say?" He asked me, shocked. I smiled, "I love you Hades." He pulled me towards him, his lips on mine. "I love you too Persephone." He then yanked off my towel and lifted me up.

My legs wrapped around his waist and he carried me over to the bed. He was quick to take off his clothes before he was between my legs. He pushed inside and I arched into him. He was bare, no condom between us and

God it was amazing. He started out slow and passionate as we kissed and just felt each other. When we came it was like something animalistic inside him woke up. He then began to pound into me. He would pull out till just his head was still inside me, before slamming into me, forcing me to take every inch of him. He held my hips right where he wanted them, giving him the best angle to go as deep as he could. He leaned down and sucked a nipple into my mouth and I buried my fingers into his hair.

I cried out as my orgasm hit me, my sex clenching around his cock, trying to milk him. He moaned and sped up his thrusting. When he came I could feel his hot semen fill me and I liked that thought of having him inside me, marking me as his. Now I know why his mood changed, he liked that thought just as much as I did. He smirked as he pulled out. He flipped me over, putting a pillow under my hips, he leaned down by my ear, "I'm not gonna stop till I know you cant walk tomorrow." That thought alone had my toes curling. I still turned my head to give him a challenging smirk, "Good luck with that." I learned quickly he was surely a man of his word.

Chapter 8

I woke up feeling sore. I felt Hades place a kiss on my shoulder. I rolled over to look at him. He had a sexy sleepy smile on his face. He gave me a soft and slow kiss. This was so different. We were more open without talking. As if confessing our love for each other so easily broke down those walls we had been keeping up. "Are you hungry, " He asked me while tucking a strand of my hair behind my ear. I nodded, "Very." He chuckled softly, before getting up. He grabbed himself a pair of boxers and sweats. He went to open the door but I cleared my throat.

He turned to look at me and I threw a shirt at him. "I don't want others to see what's mine, " I told him. He chuckled and put it on, "Yes ma'am." He left the room and I decided to take a shower. I thought about the guild, about how I was now its Master.

The door to the bathroom opened and Hades came in, "Our breakfast is waiting for us." Hades said from the doorway. I turned off the water and wrapped my towel around me. He pulled me to him and gave me a kiss, "I see you're able to walk. I should try harder next time." I laughed and rolled my eyes. Truth be told, I was a little sore but I wasn't going to let that stop me from doing what I needed to. I threw on one of his shirts and a thong before sitting on the bed to enjoy breakfast.

"So what are you going to do, " Hades asked me as he sat across from me on the bed to eat his food. I sighed, "Change the guild for the better to start." I tucked a strand of my hair behind my ear, "They're counting on me to guide them to a better life." "What will you do for your finances? Running a guild can't be cheap, " Hades pointed out to me. "We'll still kill, it's part of who we are. Instead of being assassins though, I think turning us into a protection agency is our best route. I have many powerful ties to assist with that."

He nodded, "We can create an alliance unlike any other." I smiled, "I would like that very much."

Later that day I walked into the guild house, ready to start knocking down walls. I went to the Master's office and saw it was the way it had always been, his treasure trove. I looked at the various rare items he had many of us and those who were before us, steal for him. "I used to hate you, " Ice said, leaning in the doorway. "Hated how much attention he gave you. Then you escaped this hell hole. We all envied you for it. Then I realized, it had to hurt like hell to leave." I turned to face him before I moved part of my shirt, showing the scar above my heart that peaked above my bra, "It did. Nearly killed me, but it was worth it. Although, I didn't know freedom until I met Hades."

He studied me before smiling softly. He gestured with his head for me to follow him. He took me to the dining hall and the chair at the head of the table was waiting for me. "So what is your first order of business Mistress, " Ice asked when he took his seat. "No more killing for money, " I declared. "The guild of assassins will end with our generation, and we will bring about a guild who protects. I have already started the path where we are known as a special protection agency. We will work on a more gray line of the law instead of strictly against the law. Killing will be needed here and there but safety comes first. On that note, no man gets left behind. If one of us is in deep shit, we help in any way we can. We are a family now, no more every man for themselves." They all eyed each other before looking at me. "If you have any complaints, the door is right there. I won't stop you, nor will you be hunted down, " I vowed to them. "I won't hold it against you either. We went through intense hell as kids because of our Master. I'm the Master now, and I'm breaking down old walls and putting up new ones. If you want to cut your ties, now is the time to leave before I waste my breath on you." I paused and waited. I waited a few minutes before continuing, happy they all decided to stay. "As you all know, I'm with the President of Inferno MC, Hades. We have come to an agreement to create an alliance that no one has ever seen before. Consider them your brethren, but they handle other things such as guns and money laundering while we handle protection."

"What does our protection services include, " Croft asked me.

"What a good question, " I told him. "From big names to the common family, we protect them. From stalkers to abusive family members. Never do we charge a child under the age of twenty-one, if they need our help then we give it. Any objections?" When none came, I smiled happily. "Perfect."

After that, we began discussing loose ends our Master had left behind. I was sipping a glass of wine, going over the last details when Hades called me. "Hello my underworld king, " I said with a smile. Ice rolled his eyes while a couple of the others chuckled. "Have you been drinking my goddess, " He asked me. I could hear the amusement in his voice. "A little, " I confessed.

He chuckled, "You finished your end?" "Just about. How did the brothers handle it, " I asked him while studying the wine in my glass. "They have declared me bat shit crazy, but they feel its a good step for us, " He said with a sigh. "Unfortunately, that means more paperwork." I giggled softly, "Does that mean I get to see you in those sexy glasses of yours?" Yep, I needed to stop drinking the wine before I make a fool out of myself. "I'll be there soon to pick you up, " He told me. "Try not to drink too much before I get there."

"I'll try, " I told him before hanging up. "So how does it work at their MC, " Ice asked me. "They're a group of honorable hard-asses who always have each other's backs, " I replied. My eyes went down to the tattoo on my arm, "Through thick and thin, they never back down. They have a type of craziness that compliments our own." It's why this alliance will work out beautifully.

When Hades came to pick me up, I was a little disappointed that he came in his truck. He saw my pout and shook his head as he opened the door for me. "I didn't know how much you had to drink and I didn't want you falling off the back of my bike, " He told me before kissing my cheek. I rolled my eyes as he shut the door.

He got in the driver seat and laced his fingers with mine once he started driving. "You know other MCs will come after us to try and shut us down once they hear about our alliance, " He said to me. I smirked, "Let them. I would like to see them try." He chuckled and shook his head, "You surely do put the hot in psychotic." I laughed, "Thanks for the compliment big guy." He brought my hand up to his lips and kissed it, "Any time."

Chapter 9

I sighed as I stretched my sore muscles. For hours I was going through old paperwork. The old Master surely enjoyed keeping any piece of dirt he could get his hands on to save for a rainy day. I have read so many old contracts, reports of various kinds, and even a portfolio on the many assassins that have come and gone. Apparently fifty or so of them are being considered sleeping assassins who are retired for the most part unless they were needed for a special job. I had Ice call them and inform them of the changes, to see if they would like to cut ties or join us.

There was a knock on the door, causing me to look up from the file in my hands. Set was standing in the doorway. "Hey, what's up," I asked him. I noticed the look of grief in his eyes, and it caused me to close my file. "Shut the door," I told him as I gestured to the chair across from the desk. He shut the door and sat in the chair. "I didn't know who else to talk to about this," He said as he ran a hand through his hair. "What's going on," I asked him. "Julie cheated on me with a brother," He rushed out, his shoulders sagging. To say I was in shock was an understatement. Julie is his old lady. A declaration like that is more binding than a marriage and to stray from that could get you killed in some MCs. The fact it was with a brother was even worse. Set had every right to shoot them both if he wanted to.

"How did you find out," I asked him. "I was going to go on that job with Hades, but turns out it wasn't as big as we originally thought it was going to be, so he sent me and a few others off to go do our own things. So since I was going to have the night off, I was going to take Julie out to do some dancing. I walked in on her and Haze in bed together. I didn't say anything, I just turned on my heel and left. I could hear her calling out after me, but I just left and came here," He told me. He looked so torn. Out of all of the guys, I would have never guessed Haze. Haze was a quiet man who amazing with a sniper rifle.

"What do you want to do," I asked him. "Blow their fucking brains out," He said out of anger. I noticed my office door as Hades came in. He shut it quietly as Set spoke and leaned against the wall. "You and I both know that's not what you want," I told him. He sighed and slouched in his chair, looking like a defeated man. "What should I do," He asked me. "Expose them," I told him. "If you went about declaring it happened, something tells me they'd deny it so they don't lose respect from the others."

He raised an eyebrow, "And how would I do that?" I pulled my tablet out of my bag, "I put cameras in the hallways and hangout rooms." "Does Hades know," He asked me. I nodded, "Who do you think helped me put them up?" I handed him the tablet when I found the video. You could see him walking in, then walking out a minute later. A minute after that you see Julie come out with a sheet wrapped around her body and Haze coming out of the room with his cut in hand, covering his dick.

"I can put it on a flash drive for you, and you can do with it what you want," I offered to him. He nodded and I turned to my computer and did it. I handed him the flash drive and he took it, slipping it into his pocket. "Thanks Persephone," He said softly before turning. He noticed Hades standing there. He looked down at the floor as he walked past him. Hades gave him a comforting slap on the back, "We've got your back brother." Set nodded then raised his head before shutting the door on his way out.

Hades came over to the desk with a sad smile, "I never saw that coming." "Most people hide their evil nature and show their loving side for all to see, it's what makes them such great tricksters, while you and let our evil sides show to the world while we hide the fact we know how to love," I told him. He nodded in agreement, "This is true."

Ice then came in with some papers, "Ten of them are gonna stay in retirement, but the other forty will be joining." I took the forms with a nod, "That's good to hear." I looked over the forms as Hades' phone began to ring. "Yeah," He said. He was quiet for a moment then sighed, "On our way." He hung up and I stood up, "What's going on?" "Set shared the video and Haze went ape shit," Hades said while running a hand through his hair. I took his hand and we left.

We got back to the compound and saw the common room was trashed from a fight. "Looks like we missed the fun," I commented in a whisper. Hades hid his smile, but nudged me with his arm. We saw Haze tied to a chair with the other brothers glaring at him. Julie was trying to hide herself. "I take it Set shared the video," Hades commented. "Why the fuck were there cameras," Haze spat in anger. "If anyone should be asking questions, it's me," Hades told him, his tone cold and full of authority. "You have absolutely no right to get pissed off at Set for being in possession of that video. You don't have any right to be pissed off at all. Only Set does. It was his Old Lady you were screwing. If you were a prophet I would kick you out quicker than you can blink. Instead, I'm gonna let Set decide what happens to your pathetic ass." He then turned his icy gaze to Julie. Her eyes widened in fear. "You however aren't a brother, nor are you anyone's Old Lady. I want you out with your shit in an hour." "We could work this out, right Set," Julie tried.

"I love a woman who spells trouble, but not the kind of trouble you bring. Get the fuck out of here," He spat. Her eyes welled up with tears as she went up the stairs. No one felt an ounce of pity for her. After all, she brought this upon herself. Set turned his attention back to Haze. "As for you, you lose your position as fifth seat, and drop down to the lowest seat. Want it back, you gotta earn it." He then left, making his word final. After that Haze was untied and Julie left without a fight.

Hades sighed as he plopped down onto our bed, "Just one fucking night. That's all I ask." I straddled his waist, "If you could have that one night, what would you like to do?" He placed his hands on my hips, "Go out for a drive with you and see what kind of trouble we could get into." I smiled and bent down, my lips an inch away from his, "Sounds romantic." He lifted his lips to close the gap. It was soft and told me just how tired and stressed he was. I tucked my head into the crook of his neck and fixed my legs so that I was laying on top of him. He wrapped his arms around me, holding me as close to him as he could.

We laid in silence, and I could feel him trying to relax. He has been so stressed over the rival MC and the going ons in the other chapters. On top of that we're supposed to be getting hit by another blizzard soon. Weather reporters are claiming it's going to be one of the worse blizzards in history, and he has to make sure we have enough supplies to get through it, while also making sure the compound can handle it. There was so much going on and I worried we might not have enough time to prepare for any of the dangers ahead.

Chapter 10

The blizzard was almost on top of us, and to quickly get us ready, we put the guild and Inferno together for the first time. It was tense but they worked well. Ice managed to score some really great back up generators so we wouldn't have to worry about the power. They were also able to reinforce the weaker areas and protect the windows. We had sent groups to the other chapters and they were able to fix them up and get back before it hit us.

I was doing a final check on the inventory when Hades came over and wrapped his arms around me. He tucked his face in the crook of my neck and he felt really hot. I turned in his arms and felt his forehead with my hand. He looked pale and so tired, "You look like shit." He sighed, "I feel like it." "Take your ass upstairs and go to bed, Set and I can handle everything else," I told him. "There is too much to do," he said with a shake of his head. "You're pushing yourself so much, you've made yourself sick," I told him while taking his hand.

I lead him up the stairs to our room and made him strip off his clothes and lay down. "If you get up, I will kick your ass," I warned him. I kissed his forehead as he sighed. I then went back downstairs and went over to Set. "Hades is out of commission, he's sick," I told him. He nodded, "I saw that coming. He's been pushing himself too hard." I nodded in agreement and looked over the papers on my clip board. "HQ is shut down, and we're all set up in the guest rooms," Croft informed me. I nodded, "Good. Now until this shit passes, I want you guys to just relax and be normal for once." He nodded and left and I looked back to Set. "How are you doing," I asked him. Things around the compound have been so tense since Set outed Julie for cheating with one of the brothers.

He ran a hand through his hair, "I fucking hurt, but I'm gonna be fine. Just need a woman to fuck for a little while and a good drink." I nodded then turned to look at the common room. The laid back feeling was gone, and a feeling of caution had fallen over the group. There was so much stress it was affecting everyone. We all have this feeling that Raging Bull was going to attack us soon, we just didn't know when.

Luckily when the blizzard hit, Raging Bull played it smart and spent their time preparing their own compound instead of attacking us. I went up the stairs to the room I shared with Hades and saw him asleep with an arm hanging off of the bed. I went over and kissed his forehead, hating he felt so hot. Hopefully this blizzard will give him some peace so he can get the rest he desperately needs. I cleaned up the room, and I had a weird feeling come over me. I tossed the dirty clothes in the hamper then leaned against the window frame as I stared at the start of this shit storm. Everything has changed in such a short period of time. Here I am, the Master of the guild I had run from, in love with a man who's demons play with my own, making ties every where I go. I looked over to the man who carried the weight of the world on his shoulders. He was so vulnerable and tired, all because he has so much on his plate. I want to desperately lift some of that weight off of him. He has given me so much, and I know he may think I don't owe him, but I do. I have a family, who accepts me for who I am.

I slaughtered those men in the club without batting an eye, and Hades kissed me afterwards, not caring. When I killed those men in my apartment, they were simply betting how long it would take me, not once showing an ounce of disgust. My eyes went to my girly tattoo. Every time I look at it, I smile. I can't help it. My charm bracelet shined brightly on my wrist as well. I felt like something was missing from it. Persephone, the Goddess of the Underworld, Hades Queen and wife. Did I deserve that name? I was Crimson, the assassin who enjoyed the sight of blood. Crimson was the woman who didn't know the meaning of love. Crimson was a woman who only knew how to make others suffer. The name no longer seemed to fit me. Neither did my red hair.

I was brought out of my thoughts when there was a knock on the door. I covered Hades up before going to answer it. It was Set with papers, "Everyone is accounted for at the other chapters." I took the forms and nodded, "Thanks for Set." "How is he," He asked me, gesturing with his chin. "Sleeping like a rock," I told him. "He still has a fever, but hopefully it'll break soon." He nodded, "Hopefully." He then left and I shut the door. I sat on the foot of the bed with the forms and began to look them over. Everything seemed right and in order. I went to place them on his desk and sighed when I saw how messy it was. His organized chaos, he liked to call it. I knew better than to touch it so I placed the forms on the top of the pile of papers he had.

"Persephone," I heard Hades mumble sleepily. I turned to see his eyes were cracked open slightly and he was holding his hand out to me. I stripped off my clothes before joining him. He held me tightly to him and I kissed his chest softly as he relaxed again. His soft snores a second later told me he was asleep once more. I smiled softly before letting sleep take me as well.

Chapter 11

Hades's POV

I was hoping to spend the blizzard loving on my woman instead of being sick, but unfortunately things didn't happen the way I wanted them too. Thankfully the sickness passed right before the blizzard did and I was back to feeling one hundred percent. I woke up and found my woman brushing her hair, looking like she was thinking really hard. She wore dark skinny jeans that looked like they were painted on her body, soft pink colored tank top, and the same colored pink stilettos. Her charm bracelet jingled as she brushed her hair.

"Are you okay," I asked her. She turned to me, "I don't know what to do." "About what," I asked her feeling slightly confused. "I don't like the red anymore," she told me. "Nor do I like the name Crimson." I wrapped my arms around her waist, "Then what do you like?" "Persephone, but I dont think I deserve that name. Nor do I think Crimson fits me anymore," She confessed to me. Crimson was a woman who hated the world, trying to just survive. She enjoyed hurting others and killing. Persephone is a woman who cares for many and loves me. Yet she isn't soft. She will bring hell down upon those that do her wrong.

"What color do you think best suits you," I asked her. She sighed, "I don't know." She did a quick side braid, her eyes drifting to her tank top. "I'll be happy with whatever color you pick," I told her. She smiled softly, "Good to know."

I got dressed then we went downstairs. Ice and Croft sat with their laptops and coffee. The blizzard was gone, but the roads weren't drivable yet. It was an ocean of snow outside, trapping us inside until it gets cleared. Persephone went over to them and they turned their laptops to face her. She looked over their screens then sighed and pinched the bridge of her nose with her eyes closed. "I need coffee before I deal with this shit," she said before going into the kitchen.

I followed after her. "Everything okay," I asked her. "Jobs have started popping up, which is good, but I have to go over who is best suited, and when they can even do them. The ones that are time sensitive are going to be a pain in the ass. Getting out in this weather can be done, its just a headache," she explained to me as she poured herself a cup of coffee. "I also have to look at the details, plan them, and see which ones need that special form of attention. I haven't even finished going through shit at the guild house. It's been nothing but paperwork, and none of the fun things."

I knew what she meant. Jobs have been coming in left and right for us as well. It's kept us from spending time together. Set came over with his tablet for me and I sighed. Work was never done. We worked through our respected files and such until it was late. We had been so busy working, we hadn't even noticed a team had come and cleared out the snow covering our doors, allowing us to be able to leave. I sighed and lit a cigarette. I took a drag while leaning back in my chair. A Goddess in pink stilettos came in. She smirked and straddled me in the chair.

I offered her the cigarette and she took a hit from it before reaching over to the ashtray to flick off the ashes. "I miss you," I told her. She smiled softly, "I'm right here." I took another drag with a nod, "Yes you are." We sat in silence, as we finished off the cigarette together. She then captured my lips. I groaned before returning it. My tongue invaded her mouth and she moaned softly.

We were interrupted by bullets flying through the window. We dove to the floor. Damn it, we just got this place patched up when we were attacked during Christmas! Suddenly the shots stopped and we got up. Everyone flooded down the stairs, ready for a fight. Raging bull then came in, guns at the ready. Persephone, Ice, and Croft were quick to meet them. Zenith was on the stairs, sniper rifle in hands. Not wanting my woman to have all the fun to herself, I joined them. She and I fought easily together, taking them out one by one.

When the fighting stopped, there were only a few Raging Bull members remaining. "Man, I got their blood on my new shoes," Persephone complained as she looked at her shoes. She then dug her heel into one of the guys who was still alive. He groaned. "My man bought these for me, and then you useless sacks of meat come into our home, and get them dirty."

She twirled a knife in her hand, "How should you repay me?" "I've got cash in my wallet," the guy told her. "It's yours, just don't kill me." She smirked and took his wallet from his back pocket. She opened it and removed the cash. She then took out a photo. "You have such a beautiful family. Is this why you don't want me to kill you," she asked teasingly. He nodded, "Yes ma'am." She then dug her heel in further, "But these men here have families too, yet you came here wanting to kill them. So why should I give you mercy?" His eyes widened in fear. She gave him a sadistic laugh that had me harden, "That's what I thought. I'll let you live. Under one condition, tell you President, the Queen of the Underworld has her sights set on him, and it he comes within range, I'm pulling the trigger." She then took her foot off of him, "I'm keeping this." She tucked the photo into her pocket as she walked towards me.

He got off the floor, and it was plain as day to see, that he had pissed himself. I chuckled and pulled her to me. "I'll buy you new shoes my goddess." She smiled, and I kissed her. "Get a room you psychos," Set yelled out, calling a few others to laugh. I then threw her over my shoulder, "Gladly." I took her up the stairs as she laughed. She dropped the money on the floor of our room, not caring. I put her on the bed, my lips on hers. I pulled away, "We need a shower." She laughed, "Sounds perfect to me." We had smears and droplets of blood on us, and I wanted to be the only thing on her.

In the shower as we washed, we teased each other. Unable to take her teasing anymore, I pinned her to the wall and entered her. Her moans were loud and echoed in the bathroom. I took her like a savage, my lips on hers. Her walls clamped down on me when her orgasm hit her. I then turned off the water and picked her up, my cock still deeply in her. I laid her down, no where near done with her.

Later that night she slept peacefully next me. Her head on my chest, her hair a tangled mess, and her face looking peaceful. My beautiful woman. I brushed a few strands of hair from her face. How the hell did I get so lucky? I smiled softly before falling asleep, feeling a peace settle within me.

Chapter 12

I need a day of peace with my man. The blood and gore is fun, and the paperwork was important, but damn it, I need more than just the times we have sex together. Don't get me wrong, the sex is amazing, but a relationship needs more than just sex. Today Hades was gone for a job with a few others. I got most of the jobs assigned and everyone was out taking care of them, so today I was on my own. Not wanting to be home alone, I drove Hades' truck to the hair salon. I walked in and Tyra smiled, "Hey honey, here for your usual red color?" I shook my head, "There has been a great many things happen in my life as of late, and I don't think the red fits me anymore, nor the name Crimson." She smiled as she raised an eyebrow at me, "And what name is it that you go by now?" "Persephone," I replied as I sat in the chair.

She nodded, "I know exactly what to do." For hours she worked on my hair. The end result was an amazing light pink to a dark pink ombre. "Persephone, the Goddess of Spring and Queen of the Underworld," Tyra said as she sat in the chair next to me, turning it to face me. "Does the name have anything to do with a certain leader of Inferno?" I smiled as I nodded, "It has everything to do with him." Tyra shook her head, "You have always enjoyed a bit of trouble." I shrugged, "What can I say, I'm addicted to the thrill."

When we stood, she lead me over to the shelves of products and showed me a new set of shampoo and conditioner, "We just got these in. It's not a big name like the other stuff is. It's actually made by a family who live on a farm that hand makes all of their products. I enjoy their mango scents the best." I picked up the pomegranate set and really enjoyed the scent of them, "I'll take these." She checked me out and I left.

I was walking to the truck when a bike pulled up with a very sexy looking man on the back of it. He got off the bike and walked over to me. He gave me a very deep kiss that had my toes curling in my red stilettos. "The pink suits you," Hades said against my lips. I smiled, "Glad you think so. So how did the job go?" "We scored well enough that you and I can escape for a little while and let Set and Ice take care of things for a couple of days," he replied.

All the jobs the guild had gotten were being handled, and most would take a little bit to complete. "And just where would we go," I asked him. "That my Goddess, is a surprise. Go back to the compound and pack, I'll meet you there. Make sure you pack a swim suit, and a nice dress," he told me before kissing my lips and getting back on his bike. I felt giddy with excitement.

I got back to the compound and went inside. Ice and Croft were with their laptops, blue tooth ear pieces in their ears. "Have fun," Ice said as I went up the stairs. "Let us know if a body needs to be buried," Croft threw in. I waved in acknowledgement, not wanting to stop and talk.

I had just finished packing when Hades came in, a single pink rose in his hand, "Ready?" I took it, "Let's go." He picked up my bag, and the bag he had already packed before telling me of our little getaway. Not wanting to ruin the surprise, I didn't do any snooping for some kind of hint to where it was we were going. We went to the truck and he put the bags in the back while I got in the passenger seat. I put my nose to petals of the rose, a small smile on my face.

When he began to drive, he took my hand, a smirk on his lips, "Get comfortable, it's a little bit of a drive." My curiosity peaked even more then. Just where was he taking me?

After a few hours of driving, having stopped only once to eat and go to the restroom, we pulled up to a very expensive looking resort. "I figured we both could use some relaxing," He told me. A valet took the truck and a bell hop took our bags while we went to the desk to check in. After getting our room keys we went to the elevator, ignoring the looks from the snobs who were talking in the lobby. When we got to our room I was expecting Hades to go all out. Penthouse suite at an expensive resort. He knew I hated it when he spoiled me. I guess in a way I could let it slide a little since he was also going to be enjoying the benefits. The penthouse suite also had its own hot tub on the very large balcony that over look the city. "I see you decided to go all out," I teased as I began to unpack my bag. He wrapped his arms around my waist, "Only the best for you." He pressed a soft kiss to the side of my neck. "My Goddess." I leaned into him, "So tell me, what else do you have planned for us?" "Tonight, just a nice soak in the hot tub with a drink of your choice. Tomorrow though, I plan on taking you to the carnival near by, then a nice dinner that night. Then the next day we'll enjoy the in door pool, and whatever we feel like," He shared with me. "That sounds like heaven," I told him honestly. A couple days to just be together. No raging bull. No jobs. No paper work. Just him and me.

Later in the hot tub we looked over the city, my back against his chest, a glass of wine in my hand. "What do you consider to be your dream vacation," he asked me out of no where. I smiled softly, "Why? So you can try and out do yourself?" He chuckled, "Maybe." I then thought for a moment, "Going to a tropical island with it being just the two of us, free to do as we please." I placed my glass on the side of the tub by his, "And what's yours?" "Staying in a cabin in the middle of the woods for a week or two," he replied. "Being surrounded by nature and my beautiful Goddess."

I smiled and tilted my head back to capture his lips. The kiss was slow and sweet. "I love you," he whispered against my lips. "I love you too," I whispered back. He was going to kiss me again when the fire alarm began to go off. "How much do you want to bet it was some idiot who was smoking to close to sensor," I asked as I got out. He chuckled, "Speaking from experience?" I laughed, "Maybe."

I quickly threw on one of his shirts and a pair of sweats while he grabbed some sweats and his cut. I threw a shirt at him when he went to open the door. He chuckled and put it on as we left. We stood by the truck as the crowd talked about what possibly happened. I took a drag from my cigarette, while sitting on his tailgate.

The manager stood in front of the crowd, "I'm sorry for the inconvenience ladies and gentlemen. One of the guests had been having a party that got out of hand." There were many groans and complaints. "Sounds like my kind of party," Hades whispered in my ear with a chuckle. I looked at him with a smirk, "I much prefer a private party for two." He returned my smile, "As do I."

We had to wait for permission to enter the building again, and then it was a wait to be able to use the elevator to get to our penthouse so Hades and I decided to sit in the lobby talking when a woman with graying hair and sagging cheeks that reminded me of a bull dog walked up to us. "This is a very expensive and prestigious, not a biker bar," she said while pointing fingers at my man's cut. I stood up, "Listen here lady. We're here on vacation, like everyone else. Sorry our attire and how we live isn't to your liking, but we honestly don't give a shit." She gasped, and was going to say something but the manager came over.

"Is there a problem ma'am," the manager asked while looking between us. "These delinquents are loitering in this beautiful lobby, they need to be thrown out," the woman seethed to the manager. "My apologies, but I can't do that," the manager told her. "And why is that," she snapped at him. "Because this couple has rented out our penthouse suite for the next few days, paying in advance," he answered. "Just like you, they're paying customers." He then turned to face me. "I truly am sorry for her behavior and for the long wait to get back to your room. Out of inconvenience for being dragged away from your evening in your room, the hotel would like to gift you one of our best bottles of wine." "It's no trouble," I told him. "I'm not a fan of red, but if you have a nice moscato then you can send it to our room once this madness has passed."

The manager nodded with a smile and walked away while the woman stood their gaping before her husband finally came and retrieved her. I turned and looked at Hades who sat there smirking. "You're always so calm, yet she seemed to easily get under your skin," he noted. "It's because I know what this means to you," I said while running my fingers along his cut. "You worked hard for it, and you wear it with pride. I refuse to sit by while someone tries to trash what you worked for. Plus you're my God and King, I have to help defend your crown."

He smiled and kissed my lips. When we got back to our room we saw the bottle of moscato waiting for us. This evening just keeps getting better and better, I thought when he removed his shirt. We stripped and laid on the bed, wine in hand. We talked more about our pasts and other small things we liked. We laughed and got deep. The chemistry was electrifying and thrilling. It was really great to just being able to lay there with the man I loved, naked, and being able to connect in a way that sex could never allow us to connect. By the end of our night, we laid in each other's arms, the bottle empty, and smiles on our faces as we slept.

Chapter 13

I was woken up with kisses along my spine. I smiled softly and looked over my shoulder at Hades. "Its time for breakfast," he said when he got to my ear. I smiled and stretched, "And what's on the menu this morning?" "Whatever you want," he told me. "Even you?"

He chuckled, "If you want, but just know it would take us a while to finish and we have plans." "And we wouldn't want to put your well thought out plans on hold now would we," I asked him with a smile. I got out of bed and he began to order room service as I began to look through my clothes. I decided on a pair of short black shorts, a black brallet with a red lace tank top over it. I grabbed my black heeled booties and slipped them on. I was doing my hair when the food arrived. I turned off my straightening iron before leaving the bathroom. I was greeted with the sight of Hades in only his briefs as he uncovered the plates. I bit my lip as I watched the muscles in his body move. Damn was I lucky.

After we ate and finished getting ready Hades took my hand and we went down to the lobby. That old lady from last night was there and she gave me a glare. I stuck my tongue out while smiling, holding up my middle finger. Her eyes widened at the vulgarity of it while Hades chuckled and shook his head. When we got outside I slipped on my sunglasses. A valet was outside with the truck. Hades took the keys from him and we got in.

I was filled with excitement as I saw the rollercoasters draw closer. When we got out of the truck I grabbed Hades hand eagerly, pulling him towards the carnival. I could smell the mouth watering funnel cakes and deep fried food from the parking lot. Today we weren't President of the Inferno MC or a Head Mistress of a Guild of Assassins. We were simply Hades and Persephone. Two fucked up people who wanted a single day to be normal and do things we've never had the chance to do as children.

He paid for our admission and we went in. The first place we went to was the line for the roller coaster. As we stood there, I looked around at all of the happy families, and young teen couples who walked about. Oh the joys of having a normal life, I thought. It must be nice being able to go about everyday, without having to look over your shoulder out of fear someone was going to put a bullet in the back of your skull. Then again, Hades and I didn't fear that. We welcomed any challengers who thought they could get even close. However, could I put any children we have through that kind of life?

I would have to be some kind of sadistic bitch to do that. Although, the idea of having children with Hades, wasn't a scary idea. It was one that brought me a kind of comfort and something to possibly look forward too.

"Penny for your thoughts Persephone," Hades asked me as we moved forward in the line as more people got on the recently emptied car. "My thoughts are worth so much more than a penny," I said while bumping Hades with my hip playfully. He chuckled as he nodded, "That is true." I leaned into him when he wrapped an arm around my waist. "So want to tell me what you were thinking about," He asked in my ear. "Just some things that may actually frighten the great Hades," I told him honestly. He chuckled deeply, sending a shiver of delight down my spine, "Try me." "Just some things I wouldn't mind us having in the future," I told him. "You're meaning children," he instantly guessed. I nodded, "That I am." I could feel him smile as he placed a kiss on the side of my neck, "That thought has crossed my mind a time or two. Of course it will be well after we have dealt with Corrine and Raging Bull." I smiled softly in agreement.

When it was our turn to get on the rollercoaster, Hades and I got to sit at the very front. The start up the first hill was slow, but the drop was thrilling. It was almost as fun as scaling down the side of the Empire State building while strapped to a harness. I screamed in merriment and threw my hands in the air. At the end of the ride, I was eager to see what else the carnival had in store.

Hades's POV

I should have brought her here a lot sooner. Seeing the sparkle in her eyes, not brought on by our professions in life, was a wonderous thing to see. Her smile was pure joy and it was infectious. I followed her to every spot in the carnival till we rode on everything at least once. When the sun began to set we left the carnival to go back to our suite to get ready for our reservation. I'm not one for suits and ties, but this was one of the few times where I would sport the attire while showing off my woman to the world.

When she stepped out of the bathroom wearing a body hugging black cocktail dress, I was ready to say to hell with the dinner. She wore her charm bracelet proudly and she curled her pink hair. She had black heels that were laced up her caves. She gave me a smirk, "Take a picture, it'll last longer handsome." I smiled and held out my hand, "Oh I will take plenty. She took it, lacing her fingers with mine. I pulled her from the room and we left the hotel.

At restaurant I had chosen one of their patio tables since the weather was nice and the light was perfect. Off of the patio there was a walk way that lead to a nice and lit up gazebo by the man made pond they had.

"You surely know how to make a girl feel special," she said as I pushed in her chair. I chuckled, "Only the best for my girl." I dropped a kiss on her cheek before going around and sitting across from her. A waiter came over and I noticed the man eye her, and I honestly couldn't blame him. She was a Goddess walking upon this Earth and she had chosen to be with me of all people. They could all look for all I care, as long as they kept their distance, because after all, she was mine.

As we ate and drank wine we talked and laughed so easily. After we finished our meal, we walked down the walk way, with her hugging my arm as her head rested against it. As we neared the gazebo, my heart slammed into my chest repeatedly. I had never been so terrified, not even when I took my first life.

"You okay there," she asked as she faced me. "No," I confessed to her. "To be honest, I have no fucking clue what I'm doing right now, and I pray this doesn't come to bite me in the ass." I then got down on one knee as I pulled out the little ring box. She gave a gasp of surprise as she watched me. "From the first time I saw you, I knew you were trouble, and I wanted to experience the kind of trouble you could get me into. Then we went that small amount of time without talking and I saw it as a fucking nightmare and I never want to go through that again. I don't care what name you go by be it Vixen, Crimson, or Persephone, as long as you are mine. Will you marry me?"

She didn't hesitate as to answer me with a kiss. "Yes," she said against my lips before kissing me again. I kissed her back just as passionately before pulling away to slip the ring on her finger. She will forever be mine. I was the luckiest fucker in the world.

Chapter 14

I was over the moon. We spent the rest of our vacation celebrating and fucking the day away until it was time to go home. Back to the grind of paperwork and jobs. Maybe we'll be able to finally catch a break with Corrine or Raging Bull. Something has got to fucking give so we can all just move on with our lives. I have a wedding to plan and I refuse to have to deal with this shit while I plan it.

We got back to the compound and it was like usual. The Guild was back at the Guild House and the bikers were all just lounging around. Some played pool, some drank, and some just watched TV. Only Set really noticed that we had come in. It's not like we made our arrival something grand. "Glad to see you both made it back in one piece," he said in greeting. "How were things while we were gone," Hades asked him. He shrugged, "Nothing much to comment on. Raging Bull has been oddly quiet, but that's about it."

Hades nodded before taking our bags up the stairs. I went to the kitchen to look for a snack. I smiled victoriously when I found a bag of tortilla chips and a thing of cheese dip. Set came in as I was warming up the dip. He then noticed the ring on my hand. "The bastard fucking purposed," he asked eyebrows raised. "Yep," I said happily. "Please tell me he didn't do it in some stupid ass spur of the moment thing," He said with a chuckle. "He was very romantic. He cleaned up nicely, even got on one knee," I told him. I got me a man who could do black tie and a man who could go rugged. The best of both worlds.

Hades came in as the microwave beeped, letting me know the cheese was ready. I took it out and put the bowl on a plate. "Congrats man," Set told Hades. Hades gave him a lopsided smirk, "Thanks." I grabbed the chips, "So what's next on our agenda?" "Raging Bull is having major guns shipped to them," Set told us. "Ice and Croft are ensuring the police catch them with it. We're trying to get as many of those bastards out of our hair as possible." I nodded and opened the bag of chips. Hades took one and dipped it into the cheese, "One less problem to deal with sounds great to me." "Unless those that aren't arrested come after us all pissed off," I pointed out before taking a bite out of a cheese covered chip. "Then they deserve our wraith for not heading your warning," Set threw in, grabbing a chip of his own.

We continued to talk about what could possibly happen next regarding the Raging Bull and I couldn't help but find it comical. We were standing in the kitchen eating chips with cheese dip while discussing possibly having to kill people. This was my life in a nutshell, and it was perfect.

After we finished our snack we left the kitchen and went our separate ways. I went to the Guild House to touch base with them. By now all of the ones who had been sleeping members should be settled in, and I needed to properly meet them.

Fallyn greeted me when I went in. "How was your trip," he asked me. "It was amazing and much needed. How have things been while I was gone," I asked him. "A little tense. The old members are deeming you irresponsible for having left and not greeting them properly," he answered as Zenith came in. "Thank fuck you're back. These damn geezers are getting on my damn nerves with this, back in my day bullshit," Zenith told me. "They're not geezers," I told him while rolling my eyes. The sleeping members were in their mid forties at the oldest. That didn't make them geezers.

"Could have fooled me," Zenith grumbled. I rolled my eyes, and began to make my way to the office. A man who had an eyepatch covering one eye was coming down the stairs when he spotted me. "Since when did we start letting escorts into the guild," he asked. I gave him a cold smile, "I'm your new Head Mistress, Persephone, formerly known as Crimson." "Assassins are supposed to look stealthy and blend in, not walk around looking like a beacon that says, look at me," he said, looking me up and down. "Then it's a good thing we're not assassins anymore isn't it," I asked him. "As Ice had informed you, we are changing for the better. If you have a problem with it, the door is right there." He nodded, "I'm well aware of the changes. Tell me, do these changes include you disappearing often?" "What I do and where I go during my free time, is my business, and my business alone," I told him. "And it is in your best interest to stay out of them."

"Then explain to me why we have men in cuts coming and going every now and then," He asked me. "We have an alliance with Inferno," I told him. "They have territory covering practically half the country. They have great sway with the police and other authority figures here. It would be foolish to not make an alliance with them." "And what are they expecting of us," He asked, crossing his arms. "Just our help whenever it's needed," I answered. I then stepped up to him, "I understand you're feeling lost and confused, because nothing is how it was once before, but I'm telling you this only once. Do not question me. I have so many who work for me, I could easily dispose of you and it wouldn't change a thing. I'll even do it while looking like a fucking highlighter just so that you at least see one bright thing when your pathetic life flashes before your eyes as you take your final breaths. And trust me, those breaths will be painful."

I then went to my office where a stack of paperwork was waiting for me. As I worked through my papers the members who had been retired came in one by one so we could properly meet. After that Croft and Ice came in. "How did it go," I asked them. "We got over half of their MC arrested, with enough planted on them that many will be spending life in prison. Including their President," Croft said as he sat in the chair in front of my desk.

I nodded, "Great, now we just have the problem of Corrine to deal with. Any luck tracking her down?" Ice shook his head, "We managed to find some members of the guild she used to be a part of, but no one has seen her for years. She kind of went insane after you killed her boyfriend." I rolled my eyes, "It's not like he loved her or anything. He even admitted he was just using her for her money. I did her a favor taking out that waste of space."

"She doesn't see it that way," Croft pointed out. I rolled my eyes, "Of course she doesn't." "We won't rest until we find her," Ice promised. Croft then smirked, "So how did your getaway go?" "It was wonderful," I answered with a soft smile. "Any ideas on what you want your wedding to be like," Ice asked me. I shook my head, "I don't know the first thing about planning a wedding." I never thought I would ever have to plan one. I had been an assassin, avoiding love at all costs. Now I'm in love with a man that loves and accepts me for who I am. Most of the time it feels like I dream, I just pray it doesn't turn into a nightmare.

Chapter 15

I woke up to a calling card from Corinne. I knew sooner or later the bitch would come calling, wanting to face off against me. She sent it in the form of a letter with a wax seal and everything. She explained how she had wanted to kill Hades so I could know her pain, but she knew it would just make me come after her even more. So she decided to do a simple meet up for us to have it out once and for all. She was tired of running and trying to come up with some devious plan to kill me. She wanted it to be just like how me and the love of her life had did it. He and I had a battle to the death. I had been paid to kill him, but I respected him enough to tell him. He was all for it, and wished me the best of luck. Of course in the end I had been victorious, and collecting my winnings.

"I don't like this," Hades said as he looked at me after reading the letter. "I do," I told him. "Saves me the time of having to hunt her down." "Who's to say this isn't a trap," he asked me, tossing the letter down. I shrugged, "It most likely is." "This is fucking insane Vixen," he said, anger coursing through him. It was the first time he had ever used my birth name. It had always been either Crimson or Persephone, but never Vixen. It told me he was terrified of losing me.

"I know that Fernando," I told him, looking him in the eyes. Fernando Hernandez, my Hades, the love of my life. I was beyond scared that I was going to lose him, and I would rather it be me than him. "Then why are you fucking going through with this," he snapped. "Because it's the only fucking shot I have. She's fucking brilliant at hiding her tracks, the best I've ever seen, but she isn't as good as I am when it comes to fighting and killing," I told him. "And she knows that," he told me. "It's why she's hiding and playing you like a fucking game. She doesn't want to go head to head with you. Hell, for all we know, she's not even going to show up to the meeting place, and just blow you sky high." "Then what the hell do you think I should do," I asked him.

"Use that beautiful brain of yours and out smart her," he told me. "Stop thinking like the Crimson who killed to survive on her own and start thinking like the Persephone who is wanting to protect those she loves." He then cupped my face between his hands, "I can't lose you." I melted into him. Only he could do this to me. I stepped away, sighing while running a hand through my hair. "We can use the meeting to get eyes on her, though. We'll have someone watching the area, and then track her from there. After that, we'll set up a plan." He nodded in approval, "There you go. That's better. We're going to get through this, together."

I nodded, "Together."

Later that night I was on the deck of the compound smoking a cigarette when Jakal came out. "You see where Set or Hades went," he asked me. "They went to run an errand," I told him while flicking the ashes from my cigarette, "What's up?" "I needed to give Hades that report he wanted regarding a recent job," He said while holding the file out to me. I took it, "I'll make sure he gets it." He pulled a cigarette out of his pack, "So why are you standing out here in the cold?" "Needed some fresh air," I told him. He nodded, "I get ya. Dealin' with Hades ain't easy." I laughed softly, "No he isn't. How long have you been part of the club?" "Goin' on five years now,"

He told me. "He's the reason my road name is Jakal. My real name is Ja'kal with a comma between the A and the K, but the old fuck wasn't wearing his glasses and couldn't see the comma when he read it on the paper. He then asked me why my parents named me after a dog breed. It stuck after that."

I snorted as I shook my head, "He isn't that old. He's only in his thirties." He chuckled, "Older than me, so that makes him old in my book." He flicked his ashes, "So what's he done that makes you want to get fresh air?" "Just dealing with the same shit on a different day," I told him. "It's that Corrine chick that wants you dead ain't it," he asked me. The whole club knew to be on the look out for her and to call us if they saw her. I nodded, "Yeah. She's taunting us with a meet up and Hades thinks it's a trap so he wants us to play it safe."

"He is always big on playin' it safe," he told me. "From his rules regarding himself, to the club. He's one of the best presidents we've ever had. He wants as few casualties as possible, because he cares about each and every-one of us. Especially you." I looked at the ring on my hand, "Yeah I know." "But if anything did happen to you, he'd throw caution to the wind, and unleash a hell none of us have ever seen," He told me. "He ain't got a single problem with fuckin' up someone, man or woman, for messin' with those he cares about."

Ice then came out on to the deck, "We've got a problem ma'am." "What's wrong," I asked him. "Set's in the hospital, and we could only find Hades' bike," he told me. I felt my blood run cold as I went up to my room to grab the keys to Hades' truck. I drove to the hospital and went straight to Set's room.

He was unconscious, and I knew it'd be a while before he'd be able to tell me anything. So I waited. He didn't wake up till sun rise. I got him some water to clear out his throat. "Where am I," he asked me. "The hospital," I told him. "It was her," he said softly. "She and three guys ambushed us. She said it was to make sure you met with her. They only left me alive to be the messenger."

Ice then came in with the things the police had confiscated from the scene. They had made Hades strip to ensure he didn't have a tracker on him for me to find him later. I didn't because I didn't know where to put it. I'm gonna fucking install one in his damn arm, I thought as I began to pace. "I'm sorry Persephone," Set said to me. "I couldn't protect him." I shook my head, "It's not your fault Set. You were out numbered and out gunned. Hades should've made the call to have more than just the two of you."

And he lectured me about not being fucking careful. The idiot is gonna get one of my stilettos shoved up his ass after I saved him. That's if I could save him. She took him to make a show that she has him, but it's possible she killed him and dumped him somewhere. I had no guarantee that he was even going to be alive when I met up with her. I couldn't risk not showing up, because if he is alive and I know show up, it would get him killed. There were too many scenarios and too many questions. We could try finding who she worked with to capture him, but that could take us all the way up to the time I'm supposed to meet her.

Damn it all to hell Hades, you just had to go and get kidnapped didn't you?

Chapter 16

I sat on the bed, sharpening my knives. I wore my black assassin suit. It had plenty of places to tuck away knives and poisons. It was also bullet proof and hard to cut. My hair was in a ponytail and my make up dark. I wore boots with a six inch heel, knives tucked into the sides. I would be creating a painting in her blood.

There was a knock on the door before Ice came in, "We're ready." I stood and sheathed my knives. I went down the stairs and saw every biker was unconscious. That was by design. I didn't need them getting hurt. This was between Corinne and I. Ice and Croft were only tagging along to help me carry Hades whether he was dead or alive. I prayed he was the latter and for her sake, he better be. No matter what, her death will be excruciating, but if he was alive, it won't take her as long to die like it would if he was dead.

The place she wanted to meet at was a large warehouse. The one I killed her pretty little boy friend in. I had been eighteen, but the bitch clearly didn't know how to let shit go. She spent so much time orchestrating this, that I found it pathetic. She had to get me arrested, so all of my stuff would get taken, then she had to figure out how to get leverage over me and I was the dumbass that gave her that leverage when I fell in love with Hades. Of course I don't regret a single minute with Hades. I just regret not installing a tracker into his fucking arm and not giving him the training I said I would give him. We got so busy with those damned idiots from Raging Bull, dealing with Corinne, jobs left and right, adjusting to taking over the Guild, and trying to find time for us that I couldn't fit it in anywhere.

When we pulled up, Ice and Croft stayed in the vehicle while I made my way to the warehouse, walking through the front door. Hades hung naked, suspended by chains in the center of the warehouse. His body was covered in wounds, but he was breathing. Corinne sat in a chair beside him, the cart of torture tools beside her. Her short blonde was styled and her nails well manicured. "Part of me doubted you'd come for him," she said as she stood. She walked around Hades, "I can see why you like him. He is built really well." She let her hand trail down the front of him, looking at me the entire time. She then grabbed his cock and I felt my fingers flex, wanting a knife in my hand to cut her hand off.

She let him go, a smirk on her lips, "You were a cold hearted killer, able to fuck any man then slit his throat while only wearing a smile. It's funny how love changes a person isn't it? They may us grow soft. Become pathetic." "Are you done with your little villain speech," I asked her. "I'm no villain," she said to me. "I'm an avenger." I gave her a cold smile, "You're right, I am." I then charged for her, as she pulled a pistol from the small of her back.

I easily dodged her shots. Guns were predictable. You have to aim them before you fire them. You can't just randomly fire them, praying you hit them. Aiming takes a second of calibrating. Only those skilled and properly trained in guns could hit a moving target. She wasn't trained in guns. She was trained in stealth and gathering information. I managed to get right into her face, and she drew a knife, going for my throat. I grabbed her wrist, my other hand slamming a fist into her throat. As she was shocked, I flipped her with the arm I still had in my grip. She rolled out of the way when I went to slam the heel of my boot into her.

She went to kick my legs out from under me, but I jumped out of the range of her leg sweep. We circled each other for a moment, looking for an opening. "I'm surprised you're using your bare hands," she said to me. "That's because I'm not going to kill you yet. You'll be taking his place on the chains," I told her. "The toys will come out later."

We now stood with her in front of Hades, he looked me in the eye before quickly grabbing his chains and hoisting himself to slam his feet into her, propelling her forward. My fist was ready, slamming into her face, knocking her out cold. I injected her with a poison that was too weak to kill, just keep her out of it long enough for me to deal with him. I called Ice and Croft to come in as I searched her for the key to his chains. When I got it I waited for them to come in before unlocking them so they could catch him. "Get him to the hospital, I'm gonna stay here with my new canvas," I told them, making my way to Corinne where she was unconscious on the ground.

They left us and began to cut off her clothes. She did the same to my man, fair was fair right? When she wakes up, she won't be able to move for a while, but that didn't matter. I tied her hands behind her back then broke her fingers to keep her from trying to untie it. I then tied her ankles together. I pulled up the chair and cart of tools, then sat down, patiently waiting for her to awaken. I wanted to make her scream as I sliced into her skin. I wanted to see the horror in her eyes as she realized she lost. The sadist in me needed this.

When her eyes opened I waited for her to realize what happened. "So much planning, all down the drain," I said while playing with a knife. "Such a shame really." "Crimson-" I cut her off. "It's Persephone, Queen of the Underworld, it's best you remember that when you get to hell," I told her. I laughed at the horror as she realized she still had no control of her muscles. "What did you do to my fingers," she asked me. "I broke them," I said nonchalantly as I shrugged. "Hurts like a bitch doesn't it?" I saw the answer in her eyes and I smiled. "Don't worry, that's only the beginning, it's about to get worse for you." I laughed as she began to cry and beg. "It's your own fault. You targeted the love of my life. You should have thought twice. Now you have to face the consequences."

My phone then rang. It was Hades. "Hello my king," I said when I answered. "Having fun," he asked me. "I have barely started," I told him. "She just woke up from her little nap. How are you doing?" "Nothing life threatening," he told me. "Mostly minor cuts and a minor concussion. Will you becoming home tonight?" "It all depends on how long she lasts," I told him. "I love you," he said. "I love you too," I told him. I then hung up and began to start the real fun.

Chapter 17

S he lasted two days before she finally died, and by then, you could barely recognize her. Of course I didn't spend the entire two days torturing her. When she passed out I took naps or ate a snack. Torturing a person to death was very tedious and I needed as much energy as possible. When I got home, was covered in her blood. Hades was waiting for me, the shower running. He helped remove my clothes, "Enjoy yourself?" I smiled as I nodded, "Very much. I had a lot of pent up stress that I needed to release." He took my hair down from it's ponytail. "How are you feeling," I asked him. "A little sore," He admitted. "But nothing I can't handle."

I smiled softly at him, "That's good." We then got into the shower and he helped me wash off the blood, before he pulled me to him, kissing me deeply. I moaned into him. I just spent the last two days torturing a woman to death and yet here he was kissing me like I'm some normal woman. That's what I loved the most about him. He was just as fucked up as I was. Our demons danced so beautifully together. He trailed kisses from my lips down my neck. I moaned, my fingers tangling into his hair. "I love you," he whispered against my shoulder. "I love you too," I said just as softly. He moved his head so he could look down at me. "I know I fucked up," he told me. I laughed softly, "Fucked up is an understatement my love." "I'm ready to make it up in any way you see fit my goddess," he said, a smirk on his lips.

"Once you've recovered I will be holding you captive in our room till I see fit," I told him. "For me to torture as I see fit." He groaned softly, his cock hardening as I nipped the skin on his chest. "Tease," he told me. "Next time don't get kidnapped then you won't get tortured and we'll be able to play without having to wait for you to recover," I told him as I turned off the water. He chuckled, "I promise I've learned my lesson." I smiled, "Good."

We dried off and I dressed in one of his shirts and a pair of tights so I could throw away my blood soaked clothes and get something filling to eat. I went downstairs, no one talking to me. They were all pissy that I had them all knocked out. They'll get over it. It was better this way. No casualties, plus the extra back up wasn't needed since it was just her. She had told me the men she hired were just hired help that were too scared to go against me. They were smart. Since she was dead, I didn't bother hunting down the men since they were just hired help. They only roughed Set and Hades up a bit, not like they killed them.

I tossed the clothes in the trash and went to the kitchen. Set came in, his hand in brace, some bruising around his face, "How you doing?" I smiled, "I'm doing great. Now that Raging Bull and Corinne are out of my hair I can proceed with my wedding plans. I was thinking of going with Underworld Garden as a theme." He chuckled and shook his head, "Only you."

I then made myself something to eat before going upstairs where Hades laid naked in the bed with his laptop, wearing his glasses. Damn was he tempting. Stupid Corinne for torturing him. I sat on the bed as I ate and he turned the laptop and I saw a house on the screen, "What's that?" "My wedding present to you," he answered. "Its early, I know, but I wanted us to be in a place of our own. It's between the guild and the compound so we wont be going far."

I couldn't help my soft smile as I looked at it, "I didn't think you were the white picket fence kind of man." He returned my smile, "I want it all with you. A house, yard full of kids, a dog." "No fucking mini vans," I told him. "I'm not the soccer mom kind of woman." He laughed, "I don't know. I think you'd look cute." I glared playfully, "If you get me one of those crappy mini vans, I'm running you over with it."

He laughed as he shook his head. I finished eating and we dressed so he could show me the house in person and not just on a screen. "Where did you find time to go house hunting," I asked him as we walked up the cute walk way. "When I realized I wanted to marry you I realized I wanted a home for us to grow in," he said, lacing his fingers with mine. "So I began looking. It was hard at first, but when I found this one, I knew it'd be perfect for you."

He took me inside and I loved the dark hard wood floors and large windows that let in a lot of light. It was entirely open concept with pillars that went from floor to ceiling. I loved that each one had a plug in the ceiling for me to plug Christmas lights into. I have never had the chance to decorate for any holidays, but now I could go all out if I wanted. He took me out back where there was a large pool and hot tub, and patio bar. When we went up stairs I saw that the master was on one end of the hall and the other three bedrooms were at the other end. He took me to the master bedroom and I loved it. It had a balcony that over looked the back yard.

There was two walk in closets and inside each of the closets was a special shoe closet. "A place to put your large amount of heels," He said while leaning against the closet doorway. I wrapped my arms around his neck, "I love it." He kissed me, "I'm glad."

I couldn't believe we were really doing this. I was going to marry this man who is making things I never thought possible, a reality for me. "I love you," he whispered against my lips. "I love too," I said back meaning it with every part of my heart and soul.

I woke up to the sun streaming in through the window, my beautiful little girl who was three, taking up her daddy's side of the bed due to a nightmare she had last night. Hades and I wanted to keep the Greek Gods theme going with our children, not carrying if they hated us for it later, so we named our little girl Athena. Our son who is nine years old is Ares, and I feel he very much fits it well with his destructive nature.

I pulled Athena to me and gave her cheek a raspberry to wake her up. She giggled as she tried to push me away. "Let's go find your daddy and have him make us breakfast," I said to her. She crawled out of bed and ran off, her dark curls bouncing. I followed after her and we saw Wilson sitting at the island. Wilson and his sister Ariana were twins who are sixteen, but when we found them sleeping in the park they were only ten. They had run away from their drunk mother and abusive father. The guild paid their parents a visit while Inferno worked on getting it so Hades and I could adopt them.

I ruffled Wilson's hair as I walked to the coffee maker, "Where's Hades?" "Washing the truck," Wilson said as he picked up Athena to sit in his lap. "Ares and Ariana are walking Cerberus and Nyx." Cerberus is a gray and white pitbull I rescued from a dog fighting ring when he was a few months old. Nyx is our cat who had been raised by Cerberus when the kids found her abandoned on our patio as a newborn. She now thinks she's a dog and likes to go on walks so I like to tell people I have two dogs then see the confusion when they see Nyx for the first time.

Soon Ares and Ariana came in with Nyx and Cerberus who rushed over to me when they saw me. I smiled at them and gave them some treats as Hades came in. My husband was like fine wine, getting better and better with age, and I was one lucky woman. "We have been invaded," he said as Wilson's friends Troy and Xavier came in. The three are inseparable and it's ridiculous but we love them, even though the three of them could eat an entire grocery store worth of food in one day. They were thin poles, where did they even put it all?

The three of them ran off to finish cleaning the pool and patio, wanting to get it ready for the summer, Athena following behind them. Hades had told them that if the three of them cleaned it, they could use it as much as they wanted and even have a couple of parties. They had agreed and have been working on it the last couple of days. Athena has also been doing her best to help. She mostly supervises but she's good at that. Her older brother was her favorite person, and Wilson didn't care one bit. If they were playing video games he'd let her sit in his lap. If they were all eating us out of house and home, he made sure she got some. It was cute. Wilson was a good brother to all of them to be honest.

During his Freshman year in high school Hades had to meet the principle because Wilson knocked the front tooth of the guy that cheated on Ariana and made her cry. When Ares needs help with his homework, Wilson is always the first to help him. He was their number one supporter and it made me proud.

Ariana was more of an introvert. She loved her siblings but she wanted to be alone. Unless Hades is working on the truck or bike then she is with him, wanting to help. He taught her how to change tires, spark plugs, oil, and a large number of other things. She loved to learn and be very hands on. She was a big daddy's girl, that's for sure.

Ares was my ball of energy and mass destruction. He was one I couldn't leave alone in a room. He also really loved to test my patience. If I didn't have my hair dyed pink, you'd see nothing but grays, all caused by him. He is a little terror that makes me worry for when he gets older.

Hades wrapped his arms around me, "Good morning." "Good morning," I said, leaning into him. "Will you do me a favor?" He chuckled softly, "Anything for you." I smiled, "Will you make me breakfast?" "Of course," he said before pecking my lips.

I sat at the island next to Ariana who was scrolling through Facebook, looking rather uninterested by what was on her feed. I looked at Hades, enjoying the sight of him cooking. If only I could eat him for breakfast, but unfortunately those days are postponed until we can find a kid free weekend. Our days of love making are few and far between, but he makes up for that by ensuring I can't walk for a while. Age surely hasn't slowed him down, that's for sure.

When Hades' phone began to ring he pulled out of his pocket and passed it to me. It was Ice. I answered it. "What's up," I asked him. "You should keep your phone on you woman," he said with a sigh. "We have a few jobs that just came in that you need to look over." "After breakfast I'll be there," I told him. I then hung up.

Business for the guild took off in no time. We were able to branch out and set up several guild houses. We've helped several celebrities, politicians, and your average family. When the kids asked what we did for a living, Hades was up front, he was part of a motorcycle club. He didn't tell them he was the president though. When they asked if he ever did anything illegal, he lied and told him he only worked on gathering information. He didn't tell them he was the president. I told them I ran a protection agency that helps those in need.

Hades and I aren't ashamed of our ability to kill and torture people without blinking, but we do worry about how our kids would feel if they ever found out. Hades and I also refuse to ever let them into our darker lifestyle. Our kids are so much better than us, and we want to see the good they could do. Being able to do good is not a skill either of us have, but because we know what is wrong, we feel that we could best lead our kids down the right path. There are times where we question ourselves, but that's okay, because we aren't perfect. We don't even try to be perfect.

I'm a strong believer in embracing your imperfections and owning up to them because it's those imperfections that mold you into who you are. They teach you the lessons you need to get by in life. Hades and I have learned a lot of lessons, but the biggest one we learned was that there is someone out there for all of us. Even if you're a psychopath that enjoys killing and causing others pain. You just have to keep your mind, eyes, and heart open.